BROKEN BONES

A Peggy Henderson Adventure

BROKEN
BONES

A Peggy Henderson Adventure

BROKEN BONES

A Peggy Henderson Adventure

Gina McMurchy-Barber

DUNDURN
TORONTO

Editor: Michael Carroll
Design: Jennifer Scott
Printer: Webcom

Library and Archives Canada Cataloguing in Publication

McMurchy-Barber, Gina
     Broken bones / Gina McMurchy-Barber.

(A Peggy Henderson adventure)
Issued also in electronic format.
ISBN 978-1-55488-861-0

I. Title. II. Series: McMurchy-Barber, Gina. A Peggy Henderson adventure.

PS8625.M86B76 2011   jC813'.6   C2010-906002-4

1   2   3   4   5   15   14   13   12   11

  Canada

We acknowledge the support of the **Canada Council for the Arts** and the **Ontario Arts Council** for our publishing program. We also acknowledge the financial support of the **Government of Canada** through the **Canada Book Fund** and **Livres Canada Books**, and the **Government of Ontario** through the **Ontario Book Publishers Tax Credit** program, and the **Ontario Media Development Corporation**.

Care has been taken to trace the ownership of copyright material used in this book. The author and the publisher welcome any information enabling them to rectify any references or credits in subsequent editions.

J. Kirk Howard, President

Printed and bound in Canada.
www.dundurn.com

Dundurn
3 Church Street, Suite 500
Toronto, Ontario, Canada
M5E 1M2

Gazelle Book Services Limited
White Cross Mills
High Town, Lancaster, England
LA1 4XS

Dundurn
2250 Military Road
Tonawanda, NY
U.S.A. 14150

For Cameron and Riley —
We had fun, didn't we, boys?

ACKNOWLEDGEMENTS

As in the past, I am very grateful to my friend, Victoria Bartlett, who has been my sounding board and helped me to improve this story. Colleen Polumbo, the curator of the Golden Museum, kindly helped me to locate the forgotten pioneer cemetery, provided information, and gave me access to microfiche of old local newspapers. Ms. Lindsey Oliver's M.A. thesis ("The Golden Pioneer Cemetery: Health and Mortuary Practices of the Early Pioneers 1882–1894," Site EhQf-3) was a storyteller's treasure chest that included valuable details on the burials and the archaeological excavation project conducted in the 1980s. Last, but not least, I am grateful to Riley Johnson and Cameron McMurchy-Barber for making my research trip to Golden pure joy. As boys are known to do, they found adventure and fun everywhere — atop floating logs in ponds, among wolves in a sanctuary, inside museums and historic sites, and even in long-abandoned graveyards.

The Golden Era
Golden, British Columbia,
Saturday, September 17, 1892, Ten Cents

MURDERER EXECUTED
TUESDAY LAST

William Francis Maguire, 18, hanged Friday at the Kamloops gaol for the premeditated murder of Thomas Moody. His is the third execution this year in British Columbia and should be a warning to all who might think to fool Madam Justice by taking the law into his own hands. As most readers of *The Golden Era* know, the young Maguire is not the first in his family to be convicted for murder. Like his father, he maintained he was innocent right through to his execution. While green may be the lucky colour of the Irish, it is this editor's experience that their oft-unchecked tempers lead them to see red. More often than not, it is an Irish who lands himself behind bars, or in this case at the end of a noose.

VISITING MINISTER DEPARTS

Reverend Johnson of the Presbyterian Church conducted services in Golden while his esteemed colleague, Reverend Cameron, was in Kamloops on matters pertaining to the Maguire execution. Upon his return, Reverend Cameron united in marriage his niece, Miss Rosie Heywood, to Mr. N. Murray on Saturday, September 10, at 2:00 o'clock of the afternoon.

PROLOGUE

"William Francis Maguire, if you have any last words now is the time to speak," growls the burly executioner to the young man standing before him at the top of the scaffold.

The thick, coarse rope around Will's neck feels much heavier than he imagined. His body shakes uncontrollably, and his knees are so weak that he fears they will buckle at any moment. Will looks down from the gallows at the small crowd of stoic faces staring at him, then to the trap door at his feet. He tries to speak, but the words seem caught inside his throat.

"For the last time, William Francis Maguire, do you wish to make any final remarks before you are hanged by the neck until you are dead?"

Will's heart pounds hard and fast, like a drum roll counting down the final moments of his life. Suddenly, he realizes his face is streaked with tears, but with his hands bound he cannot brush them away. This show of emotion is his final humiliation, and it angers him that the old top hats will think he is afraid. They do not understand that fear of death is only for those who have something to lose.

Finally, Will manages to clear his throat, though at first his voice is little more than a hoarse whisper.

"You think my soul is destined for hell and perhaps it is. But if God deems to punish me, then even hell could be no worse than my life these past four years.

"I was only a young lad when I came to this godforsaken land with my parents. That was when their hopes were high … and they dreamed they had found a better life for us all. But all we got were aching backs and empty bellies. And even then it was not the harsh land that broke our hearts and crushed our dreams.

"My father may have been a poor man, but he worked harder than ten. There was only one thing we needed to make our farm a success — water. But David Craig, a greedy land baron, a fraud who strutted about in his fine clothes and fancy hats pretending to be a gentleman, chose to divert the river's flow so it nourished his own fields and cattle in abundance and left ours parched and dry.

"Then our fate became sealed by stuffy men in black hats, much like you who sit here now. They turned a blind eye to what Craig had done. My father, in a state of desperation and perhaps even insanity, acted out against the blackguard. He paid for that with his freedom. Soon my mother was shunned … and my brother, sister, and I left to nearly starve to death.

"And that is why I, a lad of fourteen, left home to work twelve hours a day deep in the silver mines like a dirty little mole in the ground. I lived among wretched men with spirits poisoned by cheap whiskey, gambling, and fallen women. And though I am young, my heart turned cold and hard like the mountains of stone I pounded every day for four years." Will's voice cracks *as he chokes back sobs. "Beware to all those who think by coming out west they will fulfill their dreams — for this new land has already been poisoned by men who thirst for power.*

"You have found me guilty for the murder of Thomas Moody, a cursed human being if ever there was one. And while it is true I wished to see him in his grave, his death was his own fault. Therefore I will not leave this world without telling you one last time that you hang an innocent man."

"Liar!" shouts a husky voice from the dark shadows. "You're just as guilty as your father. You both deserve to hang."

"Silence!" bellows the executioner.

Will closes his eyes and thinks of his mother. She is the real reason his heart throbs now and for whom his tears pour forth. He can hardly bear the image of her — an old woman at the age of thirty seven now preparing to bury her eldest son.

"If there is to be no justice for me in this world, I only hope God will not fail to have mercy on my family." Will squeezes his eyes tight, fighting to keep the tears inside. "Mama," he whispers, "I am sorry for all your troubles."

"William Francis Maguire, prepare to meet your maker." The hangman's voice betrays no emotion, no pity, and no judgment. He covers Will's head with a hood that blocks out the light and fills his nostrils with the stench of someone else's sweat.

Will's teeth chatter as his body shivers uncontrollably. If he concentrates very hard, he might be able to hear his mother's calm voice inside him: "Steady, son, steady. All will be well." Her familiar and hopeful words give him more comfort than the prayer the preacher now recites.

"May the Lord have mercy on your soul, young man," says Reverend Cameron, finishing his prayer. But Will is done with this so-called man of God.

"Do it right, mister," Will whispers to the hangman from under the hood.

"Don't worry, son," replies the executioner, betraying a hint of kindness. "I'll make sure it's quick."

Although the witnesses think themselves prepared, the sudden bang of the trap door makes them jump in their seats. Then the deathly sound of neck bones snapping and the pointless gurgling gasps for air make them all cringe.

CHAPTER ONE

I was barely alive that morning when I stumbled into the kitchen and poured myself a bowl of Corn Crunch. I'd watched videos until 2:00 a.m., so my plan was to slurp my cereal quietly with my eyes nearly shut and then shuffle back to bed and sleep another two hours. It was the first long weekend since summer vacation ended, and I looked forward to having nothing to do — no rushing around, no school, no homework, no early to bed, just the bliss of nothing. But all my sleepy bliss was suddenly shattered when Uncle Stuart burst into the kitchen.

"Peggy, take a look at this — just came in the mail." Uncle Stuart shoved a newspaper clipping in my face and held it there until I sat up. My eyes were still blurry, and I had to squint to read the heading: GOLDEN'S GRAVEYARD AND HISTORICAL SITES VANDALIZED.

"Take a look at the byline." I peered closely. It read: "By Norma Johnson."

"Norma Johnson?" I said sleepily. "That's Aunt Norma."

"*Ding, ding, ding* — give that girl a prize," Uncle Stuart said. "She's a genius."

I flicked a spoonful of milk and cereal at him. Just as it landed on the floor, Aunt Margaret walked in from the backyard carrying a box full of spotted and bumpy Golden Delicious apples.

"Oops. Hi, Aunt Margaret." I winced like a little kid who'd just been caught with a hand in the cookie jar.

"Hmm, and who's going to clean that up?" My aunt wore one of her I-don't-get-this-kid expressions. At that moment Duff padded into the room and quickly licked up the spot of milk. He tentatively nibbled at the cereal, then spat it out on the floor as though the sugar-coated, lightly toasted, bleached white flour wasn't absolutely delicious.

"Look! Did you just see what your cat did, Aunt Margaret. That's disgusting. I shouldn't have to clean that up."

Aunt Margaret only sneered. "Okay, that's enough. It's much too early for this nonsense."

It was always too early or too late or too something for Aunt Margaret to get a joke.

"Aunt Norma sent us one of her stories from the newspaper and this letter," I said, quickly redirecting her attention. I was getting good at that — one of my many tricks for survival when living with Aunt Margaret.

"Oh, let's see, Stuart," Aunt Margaret chirped as she snatched the letter and clipping out of my uncle's hand.

"VANDALS DISTURB BURIAL IN PIONEER CEMETERY by Norma Johnson. Have you two already read this?"

"No, Uncle Stuart was bugging me. That's why I had to flick cereal at him to make him stop. What's it about?" I glanced at Uncle Stuart, who silently whispered, *I'll get you for that.*

"It seems someone has been vandalizing historical sites around town, and the latest disturbance was to one of the graves at some long-forgotten Pioneer Cemetery. Police are narrowing down the suspects and think it's some teenager. He could face heavy charges and up to ten thousand dollars in fines." She put the clipping on the table and started to read the letter.

My mind flashed to the burial I accidently disturbed in the backyard last summer when Uncle Stuart and I were putting in the fish pond. We were new to Crescent Beach and didn't know it was once a prehistoric First Nations fishing village.

As it turned out, finding that burial was the best thing that ever happened to me. I learned a lot about bones and how to excavate an archaeological site from Eddy, aka Dr. Edwina McKay. Even though Eddy was sort of old, a grandmother, in fact, she really knew how to relate to kids. She taught me that if you knew how to read the bones, they could tell you a lot about the past and of the people who once lived. It turned out that the guy buried in our backyard was a three-thousand-year-old carver. The most interesting artifact we found was a small carved pendant.

"What about the grave?" I asked. "Does it say what's going to happen to it?"

Aunt Margaret didn't seem to hear me and just continued to read Aunt Norma's letter aloud. "Norma says: 'The Golden Pioneer Cemetery was long forgotten by most of the residents until the 1980s. That's when some old guy dug up a skull and tried to trade it for a beer.'" She put down the letter in disgust. "Honestly, some people are beyond decency!"

"Go on," I urged. "What else does Aunt Norma say?"

"Apparently, after the human remains were disturbed, archaeologists were called in and excavated a large part of the abandoned cemetery. Soon after, the place was again forgotten — that is until just last week. Somehow the police were alerted that another pioneer burial had been disturbed. Norma says some citizens are so angry they'd almost like to string the kid up." Aunt Margaret's upper lip curled in that all-too-familiar way. "Gads, all this business of digging up burials, old bones … it's just so ghoulish."

"Especially if people go digging up bones in your backyard, right, Aunt Margaret?" I chirped.

"Particularly when it happens in my backyard!" she agreed.

Uncle Stuart ruffled my hair and smiled. "Ghoulish to you maybe, but not to a certain twelve-year-old girl."

"Nearly thirteen," I added proudly.

"Yes, I stand corrected — a certain brown-eyed girl soon to be thirteen." Uncle Stuart continued to mess up my hair until it stood on end like a witch's broom.

Aunt Margaret put the letter down on the kitchen table. "Well, that's enough of all that. Stuart, I'd like your help in getting these apples sliced up and into the freezer today."

"What?" I asked. "Is that all there is?" Aunt Margaret was ignoring me. I picked up the letter, and when I got to the part where she left off, I started to read it aloud. "'Please make sure Peggy reads my article. I thought of her the whole time I was writing it. I heard that an archaeologist will be coming to excavate the disturbed burial soon. It would be a great time for Peggy to come up and check it out herself. And, of course, she could stay with me for as long as she wants.'" I jumped off the seat and started dancing around the kitchen. "Yes, that would be so cool. I'm going to get Mom on the phone and ask if I can go and stay with Aunt Norma."

"Of course, you can't go, Peggy," Aunt Margaret said. "You've got school. And it's just like Norma to forget something like that. No, your job right now is to work hard at school and get good grades."

Zap! There it was — that familiar feeling of having the life sucked out of me. I loved Aunt Margaret, but she had a knack for crushing every ounce of a kid's excitement. I glanced at my uncle, who shrugged and offered no help.

"Maybe you can go during Christmas holidays," Aunt Margaret added brightly.

Right, I thought, *like that's gonna make me feel better.*

"Aunt Margaret," I said, "Golden's in the north where it gets really cold in the winter. First, the ground will freeze and then comes months of snow. No one will be doing any excavating in December. Besides, by then there'll be nothing left but a big hole."

That night when Mom came home from work Aunt Margaret and I pounced on her before she even knew what was happening. After she had a chance to read the letter and Aunt Norma's newspaper article she said, "I'll have to think about it, Peggy."

"Liz, you're not actually going to think about letting Peggy go up there, are you?" Aunt Margaret's voice was all squeaky and shrill, the way it got when she was appalled about something. I looked at my mother hopefully, but her face was expressionless as she reread Aunt Norma's letter.

Just then the telephone rang. "I'll get that while you three work this out," announced Uncle Stuart. It was just like him to get out of the way when things started heating up.

"Seriously, Liz, your daughter needs to keep up with her school work. Getting a good education is the most important thing she has to do." Aunt Margaret folded her arms and had that all-too-common "I'm right" look on her face.

"I agree, Margie. Peggy's education is the most important thing. But there's more ways to learn than just sitting in a classroom."

My mom was so cool. I felt like flying across the room and giving her a bear hug.

"Don't give me that line about 'alternate learning methods.' If Peggy's going to succeed academically, go on to university one day and then have a decent career, she needs to be in class every day."

"I'm not saying that learning in a traditional school setting is bad. I'm just saying that the whole world is Peggy's classroom, and yes, there are alternative ways to learn."

"Ah, sorry to interrupt," Uncle Stuart broke in. "Peggy, the phone, it's for you. It's Dr. McKay."

I glanced at Aunt Margaret, who looked as if she'd just stepped in something brown and disgusting. Then I leaped off the chair and grabbed the phone.

"Eddy! How are you? I'm so happy you called.... You're going where? ... I can't believe you know about that. My aunt just sent us a letter.... Yes, she lives in Golden.... You're going when? ... Do I want to come? Are you kidding?" I cupped the phone. "Mom, it's Eddy. Get ready for this — she's been asked by the Archaeology Branch to go up to Golden and do a historical resource assessment. Talk about coincidences! And not only that, she's going to excavate the vandalized burial in the Golden Pioneer Cemetery before the cold weather sets in. She's leaving this Wednesday and she's invited me to go up and help her."

I couldn't look at Aunt Margaret because I knew she was wearing one of her frowns — the kind that was meant to make me melt from her disapproval. Instead I just stared into Mom's smiling eyes.

These past few years had been tough on my mom. When my dad died, she was left trying to take care of me. She had a good job, but then the place closed down. That was why we had to move in with Aunt Margaret and Uncle Stuart. Now that she finally had a new job, we'd soon be able to rent a house of our own in Crescent Beach. And to be honest, as much as I loved Aunt Margaret, I was looking forward to life without her breathing down my neck every day.

Mom grinned. "Peggy, have you, Norma, and Dr. McKay been cooking this whole thing up behind our backs?"

I shook my head furiously. "Honestly, Mom, before Aunt Norma's letter came this morning, I knew nothing about the entire thing."

"Well, if you ask me —" Aunt Margaret began.

"Thank you, Margie, but I'm not asking you this time," Mom said firmly.

Oh-oh, I thought, *someone's going to pay for that.* As Aunt Margaret's face turned bright red, Uncle Stuart quietly ducked out of the room.

"No, this has to be my decision," Mom continued as she wandered to the window and stared out as though studying the clouds while Aunt Margaret's barometer edged up and steam began to pour out of her ears. "Okay, here's the deal, Peggy," Mom said finally. "You can go to Golden with Dr. McKay and stay with Aunt Norma for as long as it takes to finish the excavation. But you'll be expected to keep up with your math, spelling, and grammar."

I nodded eagerly like one of those bouncing dashboard puppies.

"And that's not all. When the excavation's complete, I expect you to write a report for your teacher on what you and Eddy learned — a history report on the life of Golden's pioneers. Now, if you can promise to do all of that, as well as help Dr. McKay, then you can go. Deal?"

"Yippee, it's a deal!" I screamed, forgetting that I was holding on to the phone. "Oh, sorry, Eddy, did I hurt your ear? I'm just so happy. Mom says I can go."

For the rest of the day I was like one of those windup toys that never stopped moving. And it only got worse after Mom called Aunt Norma to tell her I'd be coming to stay with her. After supper I reread my aunt's letter and newspaper clipping three times and even made notes.

The next day Mom took me to the bookstore and we bought a couple of math and English workbooks. I didn't even complain when we got home and Aunt Margaret handed me two more she just happened to have. Right!

On Wednesday morning Mom stood in front of me with a list. "Okay, have you packed enough socks and underwear?"

"Check."

"Did you put in five pants and five tops?"

"Check."

"A couple of warm sweaters?"

"Check."

"Good, and here's the pajamas I just washed, your raincoat, and your boots. If there's anything we forgot, you'll have to borrow it from Aunt Norma." Mom sat on the bed and smiled as though remembering something. "Gosh, I just realized the last time you stayed with Aunt Norma on your own was when you were two years old. It was before your father died and he and I had the chance to go on a company holiday to Hawaii. Norma offered to look after you. Do you remember that?"

"Ah, Mom, I was two. What's there to remember?"

Mom laughed. "Well, maybe it's just as well you don't remember. It would only embarrass you." She began stuffing my things into the backpack on my bed.

"What do you mean, it would embarrass me? What happened, anyway?"

She started doing her snorting giggle thing, which always made me laugh, too. "Oh, dear, it was so hilarious. It was the day before we were to get home from our trip and you'd gotten into Aunt Norma's preserved plums and eaten an entire jar. By night you'd pooped your way through all the diapers we'd left for her. In a small town the stores close early, so she got the idea she'd make a diaper like the Kootenay First Nations once used — leaves, cottonwood seeds, and animal hides."

At this point in the story Mom was holding her sides and barely breathing. "You've got to give her credit. If nothing else, Norma's innovative. So she went out and gathered the largest and softest leaves she had in her garden for padding your bottom, and since she didn't have any animal skin, she cut holes in a plastic bag for your legs and tied a ribbon around your waist to keep it all together. By the time we arrived, you'd pooped your way through all her spinach, collard, and kale — and, oh, your poor little bottom was covered in a rash and stained green for days." She was right. That was an embarrassing story. And between that and my mom, who was laughing like an out-of-breath hyena, I, too, was nearly rolling on the floor.

"Well, there's definitely not going to be any plums this time," I said. "But just in case, I'm putting in five more underwear."

CHAPTER TWO

By the time Eddy arrived in her old red pickup truck, it was nearly 10:00 a.m. and I'd been ready and waiting on pins and needles for two hours. But when she stepped out of the truck I nearly giggled out loud. She was wearing the same old fisherman's vest she always wore with its dozen tiny pockets that held everything an archaeologist on the go needed — a plumb bob, a measuring tape, calipers, a dental pick, string, a compass, a miniature flashlight, a small soft-bristled paintbrush, a spare set of reading glasses, a couple of zip-lock bags, a waterproof pen, and her old Swiss Army knife. But what was different about her was the wild and wiry silver hair sneaking out from under her green DON'S EXCAVATING: WE DIG PEOPLE LIKE YOU baseball cap.

I smirked. "Hi, Eddy. Get your hair done?"

She rolled her eyes and sighed. "Oh, you would have to mention it, wouldn't you? I let Mabel talk me into getting a perm the other day. I was in for my usual cut, and she said, 'Edwina, just because you go around dressed like a man all the time doesn't mean you can't look at least a little feminine.' 'What do you suggest?' I asked her. Well, that was it. She had those rollers and pins out of the drawer and into my hair faster than a camel can spit. Now look at me. I've got to go around looking like a frizzy snowball."

While Eddy spoke I began laughing … until Mom squeezed my shoulder, which was her way of saying, "Put a lid on it, kid."

"Never mind, Dr. McKay, perms are always like that the first week," Mom said. "It'll relax soon and then you'll be much happier with it."

"Well, until then this hat stays put!" Eddy gave her cap a tug. "Okay, it's getting late. I guess we'd better get going, Peggy. We'll keep in touch, Mrs. Henderson."

After throwing my suitcase into the wooden box in the back of the truck, I skipped over and gave my mom a bear hug. Then I kissed Uncle Stuart on the cheek. Finally, I turned to Aunt Margaret, who had a slight scowl on her face. "Well, Aunt Margaret, if you really don't want me to go, I guess I could stay home and do some digging in your backyard instead."

She gave me a one-sided smile. "Not a chance, Peggy. And don't plan on bringing any bones home, either."

Then she drew me in for a hug and kiss, and I couldn't say for sure, but I think she had tears in her eyes — go figure!

Soon Eddy and I were flying down the highway past Langley, Aldergrove, Chilliwack, and Hope, which was known as the gateway to the Cariboo Gold Rush Trail, the road thousands of hopeful miners took during the late nineteenth century.

"So I guess Golden got its name because it had lots of gold, right?" I said to Eddy.

"Nope. Had nothing to with gold. Do you want to hear the story?"

I nodded.

"Well, first off, I'll go back a bit. The area's been home to the Kootenay people for thousands of years. Then the first European to discover the place in 1807 was explorer and geographer David Thompson. With help from the First Nations people, he mapped out the first trade route for the North West Company. Then fifty years later those same people helped James Hector find a route for the new Canadian Pacific Railway through the Rocky Mountains. That's when the place got its first name — Kicking Horse Plains."

I was imagining a herd of broncos with their hind legs bucking into the air. "Because there were wild horses roaming the area?"

"No, that's not why. As the story goes, one morning when the group was getting ready to move out, Hector's horse kicked him in the head. It must have been a doozy, because he was unconscious for days. In fact, his Kootenay guides thought he was dead and were placing him in his grave when he fortunately regained consciousness."

"And that's how the place became known as Kicking Horse Plains," I finished for her in my storybook voice. "So do I get to count this as a history lesson? Aunt Margaret's got me keeping a work diary of all the things I learn." Eddy covered her mouth, but I could tell she was snickering. "It's not funny, Eddy. I doubt you'd be laughing if you had to keep a running record of every 'educational opportunity' that came up. Man, Aunt Margaret is such a —"

"Now be nice, Peggy. She's just trying to help."

"Okay, fine. I'll be nice, but then you have to finish the story about how the town got its name."

"Well, the first settlement appeared around 1882 as the CPR was being built. The area became the base camp for the workers and survey crew. They called it The Cache, which means 'storage place.' The Cache crew had some friendly rivalry going on with another railway crew to the east who named their camp Silver City. Not to be outdone, the residents of The Cache renamed the place Golden City. That was a pretty fancy name for a town of tents and crude shacks, which I guess is why they eventually dropped the word *city*." Eddy rolled her eyes and whistled. "But there sure wasn't much golden about the place at the start. It was a rough little town, notorious for violence and crime. They had robberies, rum-running, bar brawls, lots of gunplay that ended badly, and even murder."

As we sped along the highway, we soon left behind the familiar scene of tall cedars, maples turning orange and red, and the still-warm air of late September by the coast. Instead there were rocky slopes dotted with scruffy little pines and sagebrush, and a definite crispy coolness in the air. I could feel we were gaining altitude by the way my ears plugged up. And other clues that we were getting higher were all the warning signs we passed that said things like

CHAIN-UP AREA AHEAD and BRIDGES MAY BE ICY. I was peering down one steep, rocky bank to the churning Coquihalla River below when we zipped passed a warning sign that read: AVALANCHE AREA — DO NOT STOP. My stomach lurched, and I decided I'd better stop looking down if I wanted to keep my breakfast.

When we turned a sharp bend in the highway, a loud honking came from behind us. Eddy accidently veered toward the steep embankment.

"Eddy, watch out!" I screeched. She managed to pull the truck back just as a silver car zipped past full of teenagers.

"Drive the speed limit or get off the road, you old bat!" a passenger yelled out as they raced by.

"Learn to drive!" shouted another.

At that moment I felt like a thermometer with the red-hot mercury quickly rising. It was guys like him that made things tough for all teenagers. "Idiots!" I cursed. I waited for Eddy to agree, but she held her steady gaze on the road. A short while later we pulled into Sparrow's Gas Station.

"It's time we stretched our legs, Peggy. I'll fill the gas tank while you wash the windows."

I picked up the squeegee to start scrubbing at the splattered insects stuck to the windshield. Out of the corner of my eye I caught a glimpse of the same silver sports car parked in front of the store. The driver and his friends were standing beside it drinking Slurpees. Eddy saw them, too, and walked over. I thought, *Good. Eddy's going to blast them.*

"Hi there, boys. That car sure is something."

30

The blond driver eyed her up and down carefully. He looked as if he was thinking the same thing I was. "Yeah, 1975 Gran Torino."

"You don't say? Well, I just need to tell you that ..."

Here it comes, I thought. *She's going to let them have it.*

"It's a beautiful car, and I'm pretty sure if my grandson were here he'd be begging for a ride."

What! She wasn't blasting the kid at all — just complimenting him.

The boy's eyes softened, and he smiled. "You know, it's the same car they drove in the *Starsky and Hutch* TV show. Except, of course, it's not the same colour." He was gushing with pride now.

"That's impressive. It's the kind of car you'll want to keep forever."

The boy nodded.

"C'mon, Nathan," said the kid riding shotgun. I gotta get home."

The blond boy turned to Eddy. "Well, see ya."

"Right, see you," Eddy said. "And drive carefully, Nathan. You don't want anything to happen to that car of yours." Eddy turned and went inside to pay for her gas.

The boy waved and said something like "Have a nice day, ma'am."

"Eddy, that's the kid who almost pushed us off the road," I said when she got into the car. "Why didn't you tell him off?"

"I could've done that. And then he'd just have given some smart-aleck response and tore off full of

31

emotion. That would only have made matters worse, Peggy. I wanted to diffuse the situation. I want those boys to get home safely."

"Well, they're jerks, if you ask me."

"Might look like that. But I'll bet when they get home for dinner tonight they'll kiss their mothers, wash up the dishes afterward, and then go up to their rooms with their little league baseball trophies and stamp collections and do homework."

Eddy and I drove on through tunnels and along steep river embankments and passed fields covered in alfalfa. We also went through lots of little towns in less time than it took to blink an eye. But tiny as they were, every one of them had a little cemetery enclosed by a white picket fence.

Soon the droning of the pavement and the gentle jostling of the truck lulled me to sleep. I dozed on and off for hours, dreaming about horseshoes wedged inside skulls, scruffy miners duking it out, and oddly enough, plums and stinky diapers. But the dream that woke me up with the boiling mercury again was the one in which a silver Gran Torino spun its wheels across burials in Golden's cemetery.

"Eddy, I heard it was a teenager who was caught vandalizing historic sites and digging up graves in Golden. That's gotta rile you up, right?" Who wouldn't agree the kid was some kind of low-life who lived under a rock?

"The world is made up of billions of people who all have different personalities, experiences, and opinions, Peggy. And I suppose there's got to be just as many reasons why some are driven to destructive behaviour."

"C'mon, Eddy, what kind of an answer is that? Admit it. Anyone who goes around pushing over tombstones, or writing on monuments, or busting open a casket to steal someone's valuables has got to be worse than rotting sewage, right?"

"You have such a colourful way of putting things, Peggy. But actually I don't look at it that way. When you've been around as long as I have, you realize that not everyone who does a bad thing is a bad person. Now I agree there needs to be a consequence for those who vandalize sites or break the law in any way, but I tend to want to punish the act or the behaviour and not the person."

"Oh, please! That's such a *grown-up* response. Don't you ever want to take a person like that and pull out all their nose hairs?"

Eddy laughed. "Well, Peggy, like I said, things are never as cut and dried as they seem. For example, take the man who steals to feed his starving children."

"Eddy, we were talking about people who vandalize sites and stuff."

"Yes, well, when it comes to the individual responsible for vandalizing the old Pioneer Cemetery in Golden, I'm going to reserve my opinion until I know more about the whole matter." Eddy laughed when I shook my head. "You know, this isn't the first time that cemetery was vandalized."

That made me sit up. "Yeah, I kind of remember

now that Aunt Norma wrote something about that, but I don't know the whole story."

"Right, well, a long time ago the town's only homeless guy, old Billy Pearson, got thirsty one day — and not for milk, if you know what I mean. Billy didn't have any money, but it so happened he was one of the few people who knew about the abandoned Pioneer Cemetery. He found one of the graves and dug down until he came to the casket, smashed in the top, and removed the skull. Then he took it to the pub, set it on the bar, and asked, 'Will this get me a beer or two?' Well, the bartender gave him a beer just to keep him busy until he could get the RCMP to come."

"Did they put Billy in jail or fine him?"

"Aw, no … Billy was a simple-minded old fellow, a real character. He was the kind of guy everyone in a small town looked out for. He was charged with a misdemeanour and made to promise he'd never do it again, that's all."

I had to scratch my head at that one. I mean, where I came from, digging up someone's grave was a crime.

"Unfortunately, a while later, some teens found the old cemetery, too, and made a real mess of things. The town decided they'd better get some help, so a crew of archaeologists came and excavated a large portion of the cemetery."

I was in the middle of figuring out what I wanted to say to those subhuman teenagers when Eddy let out a yell that made me nearly jump out the window.

"*Yahoo!* It's the Last Spike!"

I stared at her and wondered if her tightly wound hair had cut off the circulation to her brain.

"Sorry if I startled you. It's just that we're coming up to one of the neatest little pieces of Canadian history. I'll show you."

We pulled off the highway and entered a parking lot with a sign that read: WELCOME TO LAST SPIKE PROVINCIAL PARK, CRAIGELLACHIE, B.C. For the next twenty minutes Eddy told me the history of the building of the railway across Canada.

"It was an amazing accomplishment," she explained. "It took thousands of labourers to build it — men who came from Italy, England, Ireland, United States, and China. Unfortunately, a lot of people suffered because of the railway, too. The Chinese were exploited and paid only half of what the Europeans got. The First Nations were forced to give up land. And the thousands of men who lost their lives or limbs were never compensated for their sacrifices."

I remembered seeing a picture in social studies of the day they hammered in the Last Spike and completed Canada's first cross-country railway — the Canadian Pacific. What I never understood was why they let some old guy named Donald A. Smith be the one to go down in history by driving in that Last Spike, especially when it took tens of thousands of men fifteen years to build the railway.

We stayed at Last Spike Park until we finished off our sandwiches and apple slices. Then we were back on the road again. It wasn't long before the light began to fade. As it got darker, stars appeared. At first there were just a few, but soon there were thousands ... maybe millions of them. The only time I'd seen anything remotely like it was at the Vancouver Planetarium where Harold, the big star projector, lit up the domed ceiling to make it look like a night sky. When you lived in the city, you only got to see the brightest stars, those few still visible despite the harsh light pollution coming from office towers, street lamps, and the orangey glow of greenhouses growing tomatoes in the winter. But no matter how many stars were in the night sky it always made me feel mushy knowing they were the same ones my ancestors had looked at, or the early pioneers before them, and even farther back, the first people who walked this land. It gave me a buzz to think how we'd all followed those same stars, wishing on them, sleeping under them. I scooched down in my seat and rested my head against the window so I could peer up at that night sky as we peeled down that black highway.

It must have been at least midnight when we finally pulled into Golden. By then my butt was numb and my eyes were blurry. Eddy found Aunt Norma's house pretty easily, probably because it was right next to the police station. When I got to the front door, there weren't any lights on, only a note. I pulled it down and read it by the truck headlights.

Hi, kiddo,

Welcome to Golden. I'm over at the newspaper office working on some last-minute news for the Saturday paper. I shouldn't be too long. Just come in and make yourself at home. We'll get caught up when I get back.

Love,
Aunt Norma

P.S. The door isn't locked — never is! In fact, the only places that get locked around here are the bank and the jail.

I turned the knob and pushed the squeaky door open, but nearly jumped off the landing when something sleek and black bolted out and skimmed past my leg. "Licorice! You startled me." I was pretty sure my aunt's cat didn't give two hoots about how I felt, though he did stop to give me a second glance before darting into the night.

My hand fumbled around the wall, searching for the light switch. When I finally flicked it on, I looked over the room and wasn't sure where I should step or put my backpack. Unlike Aunt Margaret's house, which was so clean and orderly you were afraid to sit down, Aunt Norma's place was a disaster. Mugs and newspapers were all over the coffee table, and balled-up socks, more newspapers, a cribbage board, and a box of crackers occupied the sofa. I glanced into the kitchen where dishes were piled by the sink. And there was no way to miss the musky smell that must have been cat poop mixed with kitty litter.

"I feel at home already," I pronounced, smiling.

Eddy raised her eyebrows and grinned back. "Yeah, me, too! Are you okay being here alone until your aunt gets home?"

I nodded.

"Okay, well, then I think I'm going to get on over to Mary's Motel. I'm feeling like a zombie. I'll give you a call in the morning — make that late morning!"

I watched her drive off and closed the door.

The first thing was to make a place to sit down. I moved some of the stuff off the sofa and put it on top of all the other things on the coffee table. I thought maybe I'd watch some TV until Aunt Norma came home, but after hunting around for it I finally figured out that there wasn't one. Instead the rooms were filled with neat stacks of books. They were heaped in the corner and on top of the dining room table, and along one entire wall shelves were crammed with them. The other thing I noticed was all the yellow Post-it Notes stuck randomly everywhere. I read some: "Check out what make of vehicle Brenner drives." "Council meeting Friday — bring camera." "Shopping list — cat food, dish soap, frozen corn, maple syrup." "Peggy coming Friday — get milk." She had weird quotes, too, like: "'There is nothing either good or bad, but thinking makes it so' — Shakespeare."

With no TV to watch and much too tired to read, I curled up at one end of the sofa next to some old newspapers, a cereal bowl, and a brush full of matted black cat hair. I didn't know how long I sat there waiting for Aunt Norma, but sometime later I woke and found myself stretched out on the sofa with a pillow under my head, a blanket spread over me, and all the lights out. Sleepily, I turned over and mumbled, "Night, Aunt Norma."

Out of the dark came another tired voice from the next room. "Night, Pegs. See you in the morning."

CHAPTER THREE

The first thing I noticed when I awakened the next morning was a delicious smell coming from the kitchen. As I sat up, I also saw that the coffee table was clear except for a basket of fresh fruit in the middle, the dining room table was set for breakfast, and Aunt Norma was standing at the sink washing dishes.

"Hi, Aunt Norma," I called out groggily.

She turned toward me and raised her soapy hands. "There's my girl. How did you sleep?"

I got up to give her a hug but stumbled over some hiking shoes.

"Sorry," she said. "I meant to put those away."

I threw my arms around my aunt. "That's okay. Messiness makes me feel relaxed, like I'm on holiday."

"Say no more. I've lived with your Aunt Margaret, too, you know."

We both laughed and then I gave Aunt Norma an extra-long squeeze. *"Mmmm."* I yawned and stretched my arms to the ceiling. "What smells so good?"

"I made you my favourite — cornbread. I even got some real maple syrup to slather on top." She turned to the oven and opened it wide. Inside was a pan big enough to feed ten people. "Hope you're good and hungry!"

I ate three large pieces of cornbread soaked in syrup, which might explain why my stomach soon felt as if it were stuffed with a football. I groaned happily. "Thanks. That was delicious."

"Good. I wanted something special to celebrate your visit. I'm sorry I wasn't here when you arrived last night. When I finally pulled in, it was around 2:00 a.m. and I didn't want to wake you. Good thing you're like me — able to sleep anywhere."

"Do you always work so late, Aunt Norma?"

"Only if I'm on to a scoop — that's newspaper jargon for a big story." Her voice became serious. "Over the last month there have been a number of vandalisms like the one at the Pioneer Cemetery that brought you here."

Maybe it was the fact that I was originally from a big city, but I almost snickered at the thought of vandalism being a big scoop.

As if Aunt Norma could read my mind, she added, "It's not that vandalism is so strange, though we hardly ever get any around here. It's the fact that they're all directed at historical sites and cemeteries, particularly the burials of important Golden pioneers."

"But I thought you already knew who was responsible."

She shrugged and frowned. "The police have been questioning a teenage boy in connection with the disturbed burial at the Pioneer Cemetery."

Figures it was a teenager, same as before. "If he's responsible for the Pioneer Cemetery vandalism," I said, "it has to be him who damaged the other sites, too, right?"

"It's possible, but I find it all somewhat suspicious. I mean, most teenagers don't know a thing about Golden's history and don't give two hoots, either."

"Aunt Norma, you sound more like a detective than a newspaper reporter. Why don't you let the police solve this?"

"Well, you could say we're working on the case together. I tell Skip — that's Constable Hopkins to you — what I know, and he slips me a tip or two back."

"Skip Hopkins, eh?"

"Yeah, over at the newspaper office we call him Skip Hop-and-a-Jump. Of course, nobody'd ever say that to his face — he's much too serious to take a little ribbing. You'll meet him sometime, I'm sure. But keep in mind, unless you've got time to hear the entire history of the RCMP and its predecessor, the North-West Mounted Police, don't ask him anything about his job." Aunt Norma started clearing the table. "So what time is your archaeology friend coming around?"

I got up to rinse the dishes and glanced at the clock — it was only 9:15. "Eddy said something about getting a letter of permission to excavate. So it's going to be later this morning."

Aunt Norma looked at her watch. "I hate to do it to you, kid, but I've got to get to work."

"But it's early and I just got here," I protested. "Can't you go in late?"

"Sorry, the news comes first. Why don't you wander around town and see what's up? We've got a great little museum you should check out. Henry's been the curator for the last twenty years and knows all there is to know about Golden's history. His ancestors were among the first pioneers to come here. While you and your friend are digging up the ground, Henry could be digging into some dusty old pages looking for useful information that might help you."

"Eddy told me when there's written documents available that help an archaeologist interpret the past they call it historical archaeology. Otherwise an archaeologist has to depend on just the material remains, like artifacts, human bones, or dwellings, to piece together the lives of people who lived long ago."

"That sounds like when a detective looks for clues at a crime scene," Aunt Norma added.

"Yup, an archaeologist looks for clues that can tell what people ate, how they made tools, what their homes were like, and even stuff that helps us to understand what they believed happened after death."

"I'm pretty certain you and Henry will make good friends. He loves history as much as you love archaeology. You know, some of the best information you'll ever find comes from old newspapers. He's got some at the museum. Ask him about them. They're full of information that will give you a good sense of people's attitudes in the past. There's one old guy I always get a kick out of — John Houston, editor of *The Truth*. He was a good example of how racist and intolerant people used to be."

Aunt Norma laughed. It was one of those snorting laughs, and I suddenly realized she looked and sounded just like Mom.

"The only good thing you could say," she continued, "was at least he looked down his nose at everyone equally — the Irish were the navvies, the Chinese were Chinamen, and the First Nations people, well, more often than not, they were the redskins." Aunt Norma squeezed my hand and got up from the table. "Sorry, kiddo, but I have to get ready for work."

I was about to do my best impression of a pouting kid but was interrupted by a knock at the door. When I opened it, there was Eddy grinning her curly white head off.

"I know I said it would be late morning before I got here, so I hope you don't mind that I'm early."

"Mind? It's perfect. My aunt's getting dressed right now and is about to ditch me for work. Do you want to come in and have some leftover cornbread? It's awesome." I patted my stomach.

"Thanks, but I've had my breakfast. Do you think you could get ready in a hurry?"

I smiled and saluted. "I'll get ready double quick, Captain. I'll meet you in the truck in five minutes."

It was quite amazing how fast I could dress when I had a good reason. After dragging a brush through my hair, scrubbing my teeth for ten seconds, and giving Aunt Norma a kiss on the cheek, I dashed out the door. It was only when I came to a screeching halt in front of the truck that I realized we had a visitor riding shotgun. He had long stringy black hair, a ring through his bottom lip, and black eyeliner, and when he waved, I could see he even had black nail polish. *Ugh.*

"Sorry, Peggy, you'll have to sit in the back of the cab today." Eddy directed me to the narrow bench behind the driver's seat — hardly big enough for a doll to sit on. "Peggy Henderson, meet Sam McLeod."

"Hi, Sam," I said shyly.

The guy turned and smiled slightly. "Actually, I prefer to be called Tristan, like King Arthur's knight."

Actually, why don't I just call you Frank, as in short for Frankenstein? I thought.

"It is an honour to meet the young maid of whom I have heard so much," he added.

Now that was a completely weird-the-kid-out thing to say. I turned to look out the rear window so he couldn't see how my face was turning into a ripe tomato.

Eddy chuckled. "Sam … I mean, Tristan has a flare for the dramatic."

"Ah, 'tis true, madam," he said in a phony British accent. "All the world's a stage, and all the men and women merely players."

Somebody get me a barf bag. What was Eddy thinking bringing this guy along?

"Shakespeare," Eddy said, smiling. "That line's from *As You Like It*, act 2."

"Dear lady," the kid said, "you render me nearly speechless — but not to fear, for I shall quickly recover."

Eddy slapped her leg and hooted like an owl.

"It pleases me that the lady is so familiar with the works of William Shakespeare. M'thinks we shall be fast friends indeed."

"M'thinks so, too, young sir," Eddy said, still laughing. "Nothing could be better than mixing a little Shakespeare in with your archaeology." Eddy turned to me as if she'd just remembered I was sitting in the back listening to them. "We're fortunate to have Tristan along today. He lives in Golden and is one of the few who knows exactly where the old Pioneer Cemetery is. He's going to lead us to the disturbed burial site, and that's going to save us time searching for it ourselves."

I was glad she'd finally shared her reason for bringing the Goth geek along. I was beginning to think she'd split her beam ... or cracked her noggin ... or flipped her lid. No matter what her excuse, I got the distinct feeling this wasn't going to be the kind of morning I'd been looking forward to.

Fortunately, the drive to the Pioneer Cemetery was short. After the underpass, we motored along a narrow road that ran between the railway and a steep hill.

"Stop the carriage here," Tristan suddenly directed.

When we got out, I glanced around, expecting to see something that looked like a cemetery. Besides the train tracks and the dirt road, there was nothing — well, like I said, nothing except a steep hill covered in trees, fallen rocks, and brush. I was beginning to wonder if the Shakespeare wannabe was on a mental vacation.

"Ah, Eddy, there's nothing here," I blurted with a sense of satisfaction and irritation.

"How poor are they who have not patience! Follow me, ladies."

Double ugh. Somebody get me that barf bag quick.

Tristan started up the steep slope, which was covered in scrawny pine trees and shrubs, with loose rocks that must have rolled down from the highway at the top of the hill. As Eddy and I followed him, a few bits of shattered and weathered wood caught my eye. They looked like part of an old picket fence. I couldn't think of any reason why there would be a picket fence on a steep hillside — they must have been dumped by someone too lazy to make the trip to the landfill.

When I noticed Eddy puffing like a whale, I almost laughed. She needed to come to the conclusion on her own that this Tristan guy was a git. Finally, we came to a stop.

Tristan turned and grinned. "It is here, dear ladies."

"Phew, thank goodness," Eddy said, gasping for air. "I didn't think I'd be able to go any higher." She plopped onto the ground to catch her breath.

As I looked around, I couldn't see anything that looked like a cemetery or a burial — just the same shrubs, tall grass, and scruffy trees. Well, that and a few mounds that were probably home to some pretty big rabbits. Then Tristan pulled back some tall tufts of grass to reveal a freshly dug hole about the size of a spare tire. I peered into the hole that was about forty-five centimetres deep and saw a tiny bit of flat surface peeking out that could have been wood.

"This is it? This is the burial we're here to see? How could this hillside be a cemetery?" For a split second I heard my Aunt Margaret's grating voice whining like a screeching skill saw — the way she did if she figured something was absurd. Then I realized it was just me.

"It might be strange nowadays," Eddy began, "but a century ago it took a lot of back-breaking work to clear land with only a few hand tools and the help of some horsepower. Pioneers couldn't afford to use the flat fertile land you see down there for anything but farms and ranches. But this here slope was perfect for a cemetery. It was close to the original townsite, wasn't useful for anything else … and besides that, it offered a beautiful view of the valley and mountains beyond. What better location could there be for a final resting place for the dearly departed?"

Tristan pulled down more grass and weeds so I could see a neat formation of rocks in the shape of an elliptical ring. That was when I remembered the bits of broken wood I'd seen down the hill and realized they were once part of the white picket fence that would have surrounded the cemetery — just like the fancy little fences I'd noticed around every little cemetery in every little town from Hope to Golden. It took less than a nanosecond for the heat to spread across my face again like soupy ketchup.

"Well, it looks just like any other hillside around here to me," I mumbled, somehow thinking that was an excuse for being so thick.

"That's right, which is good in a way," Eddy said. "The fact this looks like any old hillside has protected the burials in this cemetery for a long time."

"Well, it didn't protect it completely. Obviously, the creep responsible for disturbing this burial knows all about —" I stopped in mid-sentence with a disturbing question in mind for Tristan when Eddy suddenly took out her orange marking tape and wrapped a piece around a small tree.

"Peggy, I need you to find me a sturdy stick about sixty centimetres long," she ordered before I had a chance to say more. "I want to make a flag marker so we'll be able to do a survey of the site and locate it easily when we come back tomorrow."

Being cut off and ignored felt as if a bucket of cold water had been thrown into my face. If I hadn't had manners, I would have told her to get Prince Charming to fetch the stick.

Once Eddy had marked the site, she insisted I be quiet as she walked down the slope and counted off the number of paces. At the bottom of the hill she marked the bearings with her compass and then left another orange marker.

"Thanks for your help, Tristan," Eddy said. "Now we won't have any trouble finding our way to the burial tomorrow."

What? Thanks for your help ... Tristan?

Before I had a chance to say anything, Eddy marched off to the truck. "Okay, let's get going, you two. I've got to get over to the Canadian National Railway office. Since they're the owners of the land,

I need to work out an agreement with them on the conditions for the excavation and historical resource assessment."

Soon we dropped the teenage mutant off at some old house. The grass was seriously overgrown and brown, and the paint looked as if it must have started peeling off a century ago.

Before Tristan closed the truck door he hesitated. "May I ask — when shall we three meet again. In thunder, lightning, or in rain?"

Eddy snorted so loudly I jumped off the seat. "You're good. *Macbeth*, scene 1. How about coming to help us tomorrow? We could use an extra pair of hands. I'll come for you in the morning."

Tristan gave a sweeping bow. "As you wish, madam." Then he paused, probably waiting for the curtain to lower and the audience to applaud. "Parting is such sweet sorrow that I shall say good night till it be morrow."

Eddy hooted like an owl again. "*Romeo and Juliet*, act 2."

"My compliments. The lady's vast memory is my match indeed."

All right, stop the show! Somebody get this kid off the stage.

"What a goof!" I muttered half under my breath after he disappeared into the house. "C'mon, Eddy, you don't really want the guy to help us, do you?"

"Oh, he's not so bad. Methinks the lady doth protest too much."

I shot her a stabbing glare.

50

"*Hamlet*, act —"

"No more Shakespeare," I protested. "Otherwise I'm walking back to Aunt Norma's."

Eddy snickered, but we spent the rest of the drive in silence. I felt like pinching myself over the idea of having to spend the next day excavating with Tristan. I was definitely going to lose sleep over this one.

As I climbed out of the truck in front of Aunt Norma's place, Eddy handed me a large brown envelope. "Here's a little easy reading for you. And don't worry, it's not Shakespeare."

I grinned back. "Aw, that's too bad. The cat's litter box needs some fresh paper lining. So what is it?"

"Oh, just a short history of Golden and some stuff about the previous excavation. Should make good bedtime reading."

I watched as Eddy drove off in her junky old red truck. She seemed to be laughing about something — probably all the dumb things Shakespeare Boy had said. Then I glanced at the package in my hands and felt all the irritation slip away. I was eager to get my teeth into this project and knew the contents of that envelope were the gateway to an exciting adventure.

William Maguire closes his knapsack and flings it over his shoulder, being careful not to look into his mother's eyes swollen with tears. He fears just seeing them will weaken his resolve, and that must not happen. It is his job now to look after the family — Father made him promise.

"I will write as soon as I can, Mama. And I will send money along from Farwell when I get my first pay." Will briefly presses his cheek against hers and then gently touches Henry's and Emily's heads before leaving. The blank stares on their faces betray minds incapable of absorbing any more pain. How could they when their father is far away in a jail in New Westminster — nary to be seen again in their life — and the folks who were once like aunts and uncles now shun them when they go to town with Mother to buy the few scraps of food she can afford. And now this — their older brother going away, too — leaving them to work in a silver mine two days' journey from home.

There is only one other person Will wants to say goodbye to, but he dares not for the shame it might bring on her.

"Mama, if you see Rosie, tell her goodbye from me." Since Father's conviction, Will has not even seen the girl. He is not certain her feelings toward him are unchanged, and for this reason cannot bear to promise to write her.

Will plods along the road with heaviness in his heart and boots. He recalls those times he wished he could leave home on an adventure — to strike out on his own, explore the world beyond Golden. Only in his imagination he never pictured leaving quite so soon, or being so young, or having to carry the burdens of the world on his shoulders.

A sudden chilly wind comes up from behind. Will pulls up the collar on his wool coat and buries his face in the scarf his mother knitted for him last Christmas. It was made from an old sweater of Father's, and if he breathes deeply, it still smells of him.

How things have changed these past nine months since the family was all together. But even when they were all under one roof, he could not exactly say they were happy times. For, in fact, they were all nearly starving. Father made excuses that it was because an avalanche in the mountains had cut off access to the supply train from Calgary. But Will knew it was because their crops had been poor again that year — no surprise when there was barely a trickle of water running through their land. And Will knew no amount of complaining by Father had helped. The town elders knew full well that David Craig had diverted the creek from the Maguire farm, but no one would speak out against the man or lift a finger to help the family.

It was in a state of near-starvation and madness that Kenneth Maguire met David Craig on the road that fateful day in March 1888. Will should have known what frame of mind his Father was in and stopped him from leaving home. He should have been there to prevent the angry words and threats that led to the vicious fight — the fight that ended with shots fired from his father's rifle. But he did not know ... and he was not there to stop the two men, or to stop the bullet that ended one man's life and led to the imprisonment of the other.

Will's heart feels as if it is being crushed by a steel vise. He feels such despair that were it not for the promise he made to Father he would crawl into the ditch and let the icy water freeze him solid. For now he must push his misery aside and quicken his pace. If he is to make the noon-hour train, he must hurry.

CHAPTER FOUR

Perfect! Aunt Norma's car was gone, and Licorice was waiting on the porch to be let in. It was going to be just him, me, and some warmed-up cornbread drenched in syrup for lunch — and an afternoon of reading.

I was just digging into my hot lunch when the doorbell rang. I ignored it since it was just somebody for Aunt Norma and she wasn't home. A few moments later it rang again, and whoever it was held the button down until it sounded like a drill bit piercing my eardrum. When I finally flung the door open, I think I actually gasped at the sight of a stocky police officer standing on the porch. My heart went into overtime as my mind tried to figure out what possible reason there could be for him to be there — an accident with Aunt Norma? Eddy? Or was it Mom?

"Good day, young lady. You must be Norma's little niece, Peggy. I'm Constable Hopkins, your friendly RCMP officer and a friendly friend of your aunt's." He quickly tipped his hat and smiled.

That goofy gesture sent a wave of relief over me, and if I didn't know better, I'd have collapsed in a heap of laughter about the "young lady" bit and him being a "friendly friend" of my aunt's. What was that supposed to mean, anyway?

Constable Hopkins was like a souvenir statue in his wide-brimmed hat and red serge uniform buttoned to the chin. I'd seen the traditional RCMP uniform lots of times at special events or at fairs when the police rode sleek black horses in unison for the RCMP Musical Ride, but it wasn't a regular uniform, so why was he wearing it? At least I could rule out that he was an undercover cop.

Then I remembered. Aunt Norma had mentioned a police officer by the name of Hopkins. She'd also warned me not to ask questions about his job unless I was prepared for an earful of police history. So with my cornbread getting cold and this being an uninvited social call, I decided I'd wrap up the conversation quickly.

"Sorry, Officer Hopkins, my Aunt Norma isn't home right now. So maybe you can come back later."

"I had already observed that your aunt's vehicle was absent prior to approaching the premises."

Did anyone in this town speak plain English? At that moment Captain Skippy removed his hat and bowed like some old-fashioned guy in the movie *Gone with the Wind*.

"I actually came here specifically to introduce myself to the young miss. May I come in?"

This guy was way over the top for me. He almost made Son-of-Shakespeare seem normal. I had to think fast. "Sorry, my mom always told me to never let a stranger into the house when there's no adult home. Wouldn't be safe, right?" It was fun watching Constable Hopkins's face turn beet-red.

"Well, ah, yes. I can see what you may be thinking …"

"Oh, I wasn't thinking anything about you, Officer. I'm just from the city and we —"

"Ah, yes, yes, of course. It's very wise to be cautious, though we don't usually have much concern here in Golden. Being a small town and all, everybody knows each other." He backed off the porch and stood on the grass. "Well, then, I'll just speak to you from here. I understand you're assisting with the excavation at the old Pioneer Cemetery."

"That's right. I'm helping Eddy — I guess you'd probably call her Dr. McKay." Aunt Norma had said the police were questioning some kid in connection with the vandalism. Maybe Officer Hopkins could fill me in on the details. "Hey, did you guys figure out if the kid who disturbed the grave was also responsible for all the vandalism to the historical sites?"

"As a matter of fact, that's one of the reasons I came by today. The young man caught disturbing the grave, and who I believe is responsible for the other damage done to local historic sites, is Sam McLeod."

"No way! You mean that Tristan kid? Oh, man, I had a feeling about him. I mean, you just have to look at him to know there's something ugly going on. Eddy invited him to help us this morning. I'd better get on the phone and tell her."

"That won't be necessary. Dr. McKay already knows about the boy. In fact, it was her idea to let him do community service instead of taking punitive measures." Skip Hop-and-a-Jump's face looked as if he'd just eaten a sour grape. "I can understand such action for a first-time criminal, but this boy is a juvenile delinquent and is known to the police. Last year he stole a car from Burt's Auto, then a bicycle pump from the hardware store, and eggs from Widow Munro's chicken coop. So you can understand why I'm anxious and determined to bring this criminal activity to an end."

I was finding it hard to believe that Eddy had brought this teenage criminal along on our excavation and didn't even tell me about it. Why would she even want someone like Son of Frankenstein around in the first place?

"I'm sure it's no accident that a boy who behaves like a monster chooses to dress like one, too," Officer Skippy said as if reading my mind. "Nevertheless, there will always be the bleeding hearts, like Dr. McKay, who will say it's not the boy's fault that he's a delinquent. They say it's the father's fault for leaving the family, or the mother's for being an alcoholic. But that kind of logic only gives boys like him permission to go out and break the law and not be held responsible. I mean, really, who doesn't have past personal tragedies?"

While I had the feeling Skippy had some loose screws, and I'd normally hate to be on the same side as the old fuddy-duddy, I had to agree that he was right about Tristan. I mean, I didn't have a dad, and I was almost a teenager, too, and there was no way I'd break the law or destroy other people's property.

"Youths today have just got to stop blaming everything on others and take responsibility for their own behaviour," Officer Skippy continued. "And offering them community service in exchange for jail time ... well, as I see it, that's just delaying the inevitable." He rolled his eyes and made the "crazy" gesture. "On the other hand, by the peculiar way the boy talks and behaves, it's possible he's suffering from mental illness, if you get my drift."

Yup, I could imagine Skippy would know something about mental illness all right.

"In any case, the most important thing is for us to watch him like a hawk. So I'm here to ask for your help with a little undercover operation, Peggy, something between just you and me. Now if you see him do anything suspicious — I mean anything at all — I want you to let me know immediately. Will you do that? Not for me, Peggy. Do it for the greater good of the community."

A little snort snuck out from my lips. Man, this guy was corny. At the same time I was feeling pretty hot under the collar. What I wanted was to get rid of Officer Skippy so I could figure out what I wanted to do about it all.

"Sure, I'll let you know if I see anything, Officer. Well, I've got to go now. See you later."

I was closing the door when Skip Hop-and-a-Jump turned bashfully red and cleared his throat. "Ah, well, now that we've concluded the business portion of my visit, there was just one more matter I'd very much like your opinion on, but it's of a personal nature. Your aunt, that is, Miss Norma, has made a very good impression on me. And I, ah, I'd like to get her something to show my esteem. I thought perhaps you knew what kind of —" he nervously cleared his throat again "— perfume or scents please her."

I felt a howl inside that I really wanted to let loose, but I bit my tongue instead. Perfume? I doubted Aunt Norma even knew what it was.

"Well, I don't have a clue what kind of perfume she likes, Officer Hopkins. But if it's 'pleasing scents' you're into, I know something you can get her." I nearly sniggered when his eyes widened like a mutt waiting for the last bite of a hot dog. "This place smells awful wicked from Aunt Norma's litter box, well, not her litter box, her cat's. So how about getting her some nice air freshener? You can get all sorts of candles and plug-ins these days that smell like apple pie or meadow flowers or pine trees …" I stopped when I noticed that Hoppy's mouth was hanging open as if I'd just said something completely off the wall. Right, like his idea was any better? I mean, please, just how useful was perfume, anyway?

"Ah … well, thank you. I'll give your suggestion some thought." He cleared his throat one last time and pulled down on his tunic to flatten it out. I thought for a moment he was going to salute me, but he just tipped his hat. "It was nice to meet you, miss. And remember, if you see or hear of that boy doing anything suspicious, let me know."

I gave a little nod and closed the door while holding back a bellyful of giggles. Then I was struck

by a dreadful thought — was Aunt Norma as interested in Skip Hop-and-a-Jump as he was in her? Nah,
couldn't be. Could it?

Sadly, by the time I got back to my cornbread, it
was cold and mushy. I dumped it in the garbage and
went on a hunt through Aunt Norma's cupboards
for something else remotely edible. I found some
dried-up bread, three empty cereal boxes, and an
unopened jar of prunes. Prunes! Right, I might have
gone for them when I was two, but there was no way
I was going to eat them now. I settled for old crackers and peanut butter.

I finally sat down on the sofa and opened the large
brown envelope from Eddy. Inside was a copy of the
archaeology report done in the late 1980s. There
was also a history book called *Golden Memories*. It
was stuffed with bits of notes and copies of old newspaper clippings — some dated as far back as 1888.

Most of the time this was the kind of stuff I
loved getting into, but I was still mad at Eddy for
not telling me the truth about Tristan. Every time
I'd start in to read I'd get sidetracked again. I tried
some tricks to help me forget about it, like rearrang-
ing the throw pillows on the sofa, teasing Licorice
with an old sock, and then making myself a cup of
hot chocolate. It wasn't until I got out a pencil and
paper and started making notes that I finally forgot about Tristan and focused on all the cool stuff
in the archaeology report. That was a trick Mom
had taught me. She'd said making notes helped her
when her mind wanted to wander. Soon I was diving

into descriptions of decaying teeth, broken bones, smashed skulls — gruesome, you bet, and completely awesome, too!

I learned that in 1988 archaeologists excavated fifteen graves in the Pioneer Cemetery. A few were little kids — now that was kind of sad — but most were men who had died in some pretty rough accidents. Like the guy with the ten-centimetre crack on the back of his skull wide enough to post letters through, or the one whose spine was crushed, or the other who had a big bullet-sized hole in his face. Besides all the broken bones, there were transverse lines caused by undernourishment, abscessed molars that must have felt like sucking on a golf ball, and five cases where long bones had large gashes, the kind left by wayward knives and axes. It wasn't exactly funny, but I couldn't help snorting to myself when I thought about what Eddy had said when she handed the package to me.

"Bedtime reading?" I muttered out loud. "Right. What was she thinking?" She sure wasn't kidding when she'd said Golden used to be a rough place to live and bad for the health. It made the scariest neighbourhoods in Vancouver look like playgrounds for kindergarteners.

After a while I picked up *Golden Memories* and flipped through the pages, glancing at old photos of people and buildings from long ago. It explained about the local First Nations and the explorer David Thompson. There was stuff about the Canadian Pacific Railway, too, and the mining for silver and gold.

I couldn't help noticing that for a town with only a couple of thousand people they sure had a lot of murders. Like this guy named Archer, who was shot in 1888, the day after he was released from jail. And the painter who killed some guy called the Banjo Kid over a girl in the saloon. And even the son of the town's Sheriff Redgrave shot an Irishman by the name of John Barr in the face. The two were having a fight over which nationality was stronger, the English or the Irish. Then I recalled the skull mentioned in the archaeology report of the guy with the hole at the right of the nasal passage. Maybe that was the same guy.

Kind of ironic that Golden was named the "Town of Opportunity." Boy, they'd gotten that right — the town of opportunity for anyone wanting to go into the undertaker business.

Another story that caught my imagination was the one about Dead Man's Hill. In 1884 two miners were robbed of $4,000 and then murdered. Two Native guys were accused of the crime and put in jail. Then Chief Isadore came along with a whole bunch of Native braves and broke them out. That scared a lot of the settlers, so Sir John A. Macdonald sent Sam Steele and the North-West Mounted Police to settle the problem.

I remembered learning about Sam Steele in school. He was the guy who made the Mounted Police and their red serge jackets and wide-brimmed hats a Canadian icon. In the old movies it was Steele who always rode in on a tall black horse to save the day. Nowadays the RCMP still wore the same uniform for special events. I suddenly realized why Constable Skippy had been all dressed up. The word *courting* came to mind. *Gross!*

An hour or so into all this I started yawning, and no matter how hard I tried I couldn't stop myself from sinking lower and lower. It felt as if I were melting into the sofa — just like Licorice, who was curled up at the other end and snoring. I guess it was the long drive and all the excitement catching up with me. As my eyes began to close, the old book slipped off my lap and out fell all of the old newspaper clippings. Sleepily, I glanced at one: *The Truth*, Donald, British Columbia, Friday, June 30, 1888. PRISONER SENTENCED FOR LIFE — now that sounded juicy. But there was no way I was going to be able to read about it just then. I yawned heavily and finally closed my eyes. The last thing I remembered thinking about was the burial we were going to excavate. Who was it? Would there be some cool stuff like a smashed skull, bullet holes, or broken bones? *Mmmm*, I could hardly wait …

Tonight Will feels so tired he can hardly stand as he waits in line for supper. Sour-smelling men who have no patience for a boy push and jostle him along. Reaching over him, they grab at the food piled on the counter and fill their plates to overflowing.

"Get out of the way, boy, or I'll throw your skinny arse out in the mud," barks one old miner. "If you're

going to do a man's work, then you'd better act like a man. And don't you go a-lookin' at me with those sad little girlie eyes, neither, or I swear I'll smash that sissy face of yours into the dirt."

Will quickly looks away and then fills his plate with deer stew and three biscuits and finds himself a place in the corner far from the others. It was a hard day — even harder than usual — and he has no stamina to face the jeers of the other miners tonight. Nowadays, there is only one part of his whole body that never feels pain anymore — his stomach. But having plenty of food is the only good thing he can say about his life — that and the satisfaction he feels knowing that the money he sends home each week is taking care of his family.

But Will would trade his full belly for a hungry one in a heartbeat if only he could turn back the clock ... if he could change what he had done that cold winter day three years ago. It started when he arrogantly declared to his mother he would never eat another boiled potato.

"I'm going to do what Father should have done a long time ago and get some decent food for the family." Thinking of what he had said still makes his face flush with shame.

Perhaps if he was in a forgiving mood he would admit it was the hunger that had spoken that day. He was just a poor unfortunate boy whose bones and belly ached for real food. And even worse, he hated to see little Henry and Mary so weak and pale. But he was not about to forgive himself — not now, not ever. He had allowed his hunger to make him go against his *father, to go to town and borrow money from David Craig, the same man who had destroyed his parents' dream of successfully farming their own land. And what was worse, after all was said and done, the blood money bought them only enough food to last two weeks, but enough heartache to last a lifetime.*

Will still remembers the look on their faces when he came into the house with a satchel full of flour, a little sugar and salt, two small pork rounds, lard, beans, and rice, even mint toffees for Henry and Mary. It was the only time any of them had been happy in months, and for a short while he felt like a hero.

But when his parents pressed him to tell how he had gotten the food, his father exploded with anger. That night, as the family had their first real meal in weeks, Father refused to eat anything. He just stared beyond Will into empty space. Only the little ones took no notice of his disposition and gobbled every bite until their tummies were happily full.

That was the last evening Father was a free man, for it was the next day that he and David Craig met on the road to town. When Craig gloated over Will's debt to him, Father — starved and half-crazed — had no power to control his anger. At first only sharp words were spoken, then the two men broke into a shoving match that soon turned into blows to the body and finally ended in gunshots.

When Father returned with Sheriff Redgrave and his deputies to the scene an hour later, there was still smouldering gun powder rising out of the dead man's clothing in the two places he had been shot at close range. The sheriff called it manslaughter and charged Will's father with second-degree murder.

Will nearly chokes on the deer meat stew. To think it was for a plateful of food like this that made him betray his father. He buries his face in his arm while his heart throbs with pain. If only he had not borrowed money from the man who had ruined their lives. If only he had not brought food into the house like some hero when Father himself could provide nothing more than potatoes. Will's body heaves now under the memory of it.

"Ah, is the young lad missing his mama?" Suddenly, the tent is filled with a burst of raunchy laughter from a group of men looking over at Will. "You Irish — what a bunch of sissies you all are."

Not tonight, Will silently pleads. He regularly tolerates the jeers of Thomas Moody, but he cannot bear to hear them now. Suddenly, the man knocks Will's dinner plate out from his hands, and he watches it land upside down on the floor beside him. Although only a moment before he was weak with sorrow and fatigue, he now jumps to his feet like a leopard and faces his black-bearded persecutor.

"I have done nothing to you, Thomas Moody. And I am telling you, do not harass me tonight."

The older man's laughter is forced and wicked. He is easily twice Will's size, and the lad is no match for him. "Do you hear that, fellows? The convict's son is warning me. And he says he's done nothing to me." He spits on the floor and glares at Will. "I'll tell you what you've done. You were born, that's what you've done. You were born Irish and even worse a Maguire. And *like your old man, you're nothing more than a lazy job thief taking food out of the mouths of real men."*

Will's blood throbs in his veins, and he can feel it pulsating in his clenched fists. "You leave my father out of it. You never even knew him." He clenches his teeth like a mean-spirited guard dog.

"Oh, I knew your old man, all right. I worked the rails with him in '81. It was him that got me kicked off The Cache crew. And for what? For cheating in a card game, that's all. Now be honest, boys, which one of you has never done the same on a lonely night in the saloon after a few pints?"

They all happily grumble in agreement.

"It was me and Keno Jack paired up against a couple of gold miners. We took them for everything they had and would have gotten away with it if it weren't for that loudmouth Maguire. Old Mother Mackenzie had to save Jack's life after one of those miners shot him in the chest for springing a cold deck in poker." Moody slaps his leg and howls.

"But now that self-righteous navvie has got himself thrown in jail for life." Moody roars again. "What do ya say, boys? Ain't that justice? That Bible-thumping preacher gone and murdered a man, and I hear that David Craig was an upstanding citizen, too — not the likes of us." There are more gales of laughter from Moody and the other men. "Now that's justice for you."

The crass and dirty man turns his back on Will, satisfied he has milked as much of a good time as he can from the boy. But Will's blood is past the boiling point, and before he has time to think, he pounces on Moody's *back and slams his fists down on the other's head. "You keep your mouth shut about my father, you hear? You keep that flippin' gob hole of yours shut."*

Will only manages to get in one good blow, for the other man is not only a head taller but a great deal heavier. A moment later the boy is down on the floor, his body curled defensively and his arms wrapped around his head. By the power behind every kick and punch, he knows things will end poorly for him. The last thing he hears is the sound of twigs snapping — yet it is coming from inside his chest. Then pain sears through his body like an electrical shock.

The Truth
Donald, British Columbia,
Saturday, June 30, 1888, Ten Cents

PRISONER SENTENCED FOR LIFE

This week Kenneth Maguire of Golden was tried in Kamloops for killing David Craig on 27th of July last. The jury brought in a verdict of manslaughter, and the judge sentenced him to imprisonment for life. After the sentence, the prisoner broke out and hurled a torrent of abuse at several of the witnesses, invoking the wrath of God. Maguire had to be dragged from the courtroom to the jail. Maguire has a wife and three children, and a failing farm.

EDITORIAL NOTES

The present population of Donald is largely made up of single men who have no particular love for the Chinese and would gladly patronize a white laundry were it here to do their work promptly and satisfactorily. This is not written for a "Chinese Must Go" manifesto, but merely to show that there is a business here awaiting the right kind of a man to take hold of it. Donald's Chinese population are of no benefit to a newspaper, here or elsewhere; or, for that matter, are of no benefit or advantage to any businessman in Donald.

COMPLAINT FROM A READER

The Truth was admonished by a leading citizen of Golden not to boom her town, but to tell the truth about it. Here goes: Golden is the dullest town in North America, not excepting Calgary.

CHAPTER FIVE

"Do you know what Constable Skippy told me?" I asked Aunt Norma the next morning over breakfast.

"Peggy, his name is Skip, but for you it's Officer Hopkins," she gently scolded. "So when were you talking to him?"

"Yesterday. Did you know Officer Skip Hop-and-a-Jump has a serious crush on you? He wanted to know what kind of perfume you liked." I snorted, but Aunt Norma's face got all rosy as she smiled. I couldn't tell if that was a good sign or not. "He said you'd made a good impression on him and he wanted to give you something to show his 'esteem' for you. I almost gagged."

"So that's what he's up to. He's been fishing about for information at the office, too. Well what did you tell him?"

"How would I know what kind of perfume you like?" Just then Licorice rubbed my leg on his way to the litter box. "I did give him some other useful suggestions, though. Anyway, that wasn't the only reason for his visit."

"Oh? Why else did he come by? I hope it wasn't about that ticket I refuse to pay for parking out front of the hospital. I told him that was an emergency and no one should have to —"

"Actually, he wants me to help him spy on the Grim Reaper of Historic Sites — Sam McKay, otherwise known as Tristan, a knight of King Arthur." I chuckled at the thought of King Arthur's knights ransacking a local graveyard. It would have been "off with his head" back in those days.

Aunt Norma looked annoyed. "He wants you to spy for him?"

"It's because Eddy invited the creepy criminal to help us with the excavation. I knew the kid was trouble when I first set eyes on him, too — all that black eye makeup, the ghoulish stuff he wears, and the ridiculous way he talks in lines from Shakespeare plays. Boy, was I steamed when I found out from old Skippy — *oops*, Officer Hopkins — that he was the kid responsible for all the trouble in the first place."

"I can't believe he told you about Sam," Aunt Norma said, frowning. "In fact, I'm really ticked off with him for that." She got up from the table and started clattering the dishes loudly as she stacked them and then banged them down next to the sink. She was now in one of those foul moods that not even a bottle of perfume could sweeten. "Sometimes that man infuriates me. He acts like everything in the world is either black or white. And even though I told him things may not be as they seem, he just won't listen. I'm certain it's just a matter of time and we'll get to the bottom of all this. But Skip just wants to shoot first and ask questions later. One thing's for sure. I know I'm going to like your Dr. McKay very much.

At least she's not the type to judge a book by its cover — something you and Skip should learn from her."

Now that hurt. Being lumped in with stuffy old Officer Hopkins was definitely a low blow.

Eddy arrived soon after my aunt left for work. I was glad she hadn't picked up Sir Shakespeare yet. It meant I'd get the front seat and also have time to tell her what I thought about Tristan helping us to excavate. It was crazy even letting him come near the very same grave he'd been trying to destroy just a week ago. But before I had a chance to say anything she got the jump on me.

"Peggy, there's something I need to tell you about Sam ... I mean, Tristan. I didn't tell you before because I wanted you to give him a chance to leave the past behind and meet him without judgment."

Judgment? There was that word again. Just what were Aunt Norma and Eddy insinuating? I was a pretty fair judge of people ... I thought.

"The reason he knew exactly where to find the disturbed burial is —"

"Because he's the one who dug it up in the first place," I interrupted.

Eddy quickly glanced at me as I gloated over stealing away her chance to surprise me with the news. "Yes, that's right. How did you know?"

"At first it was just a gut instinct, but then I got a little visit from my Aunt Norma's admirer — Constable Hopkins."

Eddy pursed her lips and let out a raspberry that sounded like a cow passing wind.

"And I've got to admit, Eddy, I was pretty ticked when I found out, too. Just what were you thinking letting this guy — who obviously has no respect for his town's historical landmarks and people — come and work with you ... with us? I mean, we're talking about someone who broke the law, who went all over Golden vandalizing sites and disintegrating burials."

"You mean desecrating burials?"

"Whatever. The point is, why would you let a guy like that have anything to do with our excavation?" I crossed my arms, satisfied that I was in the right. Then I saw Aunt Margaret in my mind again, and that made my face turn pink.

Instead of reacting to what I'd said, Eddy smiled calmly in her all-knowing grandmotherly way. "Peggy, it might be hard for you to understand right now, but not everything in life is as it seems."

I was beginning to wonder if Eddy and Aunt Norma had been talking. Not only was it the second time that morning I'd been accused of being judgmental, it was the second time I'd been told things weren't as they appeared.

"I don't know what made Tristan do what he did," Eddy continued, "but I do know that usually when young people behave badly it's either because they don't know any better or they're reacting to something that's happened to them. As an adult, it's my job to help guide young people in the right direction in whatever way possible. And while it's true that Tristan was caught vandalizing the pioneer burial, it hasn't been proven that he's responsible for the other vandalism."

"Well, it seems pretty obvious to me that if he was caught digging up the burial, he's likely responsible for all the other stuff, too. It's just a matter of putting two and two together."

"That's a dangerous assumption, Peggy. It's exactly that kind of jumping to conclusions that leads to false accusations and even causes mob mentality."

"Mob mentality?"

"Yes, when people get all whipped up and make decisions about someone based on emotional responses rather than logic and proof. It's in this irrational state that people take the law into their own hands. Our legal system has evolved into what we have today to avoid such rash judgment. And that's why we've done away with capital punishment, too."

I smirked. "Capital punishment? That's when they made you sit in a corner and recite all of Canada's capital cities, right?"

"Very funny. I'm talking about the death penalty."

I ran my fingers across my throat like a blade. "You mean like when they used the guillotine to chop off people's heads or the electric chair to fry their brains?"

Eddy cringed and shook her head. "Fortunately, we've never gone in for that sort of capital punishment. In Canada the only form of execution has been hanging for cases of premeditated murder. Not that hanging is somehow a better form of punishment than the others. As far as I'm concerned, they were all inhumane. The last two hangings in Canada took place on December 11, 1962. It took the government until July 14, 1976, though, to finally eliminate the death sentence from our Criminal Code."

"Boy, Eddy, all this heavy talk about capital punishment. It's not like I'm suggesting Tristan be hanged for his crimes, but he should be punished somehow. Right? I mean, what about being criminally charged and fined up to $10,000?"

"Yes, about that ... Speaking on behalf of the Provincial Archaeology Branch, I told the police we would consider dropping all charges if Tristan was willing to make retribution by helping us with the excavation. Who knows what this experience will teach him? Don't forget. It wasn't that long ago that a certain young lady needed to learn a lesson or two about preserving our past for the future."

My cheeks felt as if they were being pinched red. I'd somehow managed to forget about the time I almost sold an ancient Coast Salish artifact so I could get back at my Aunt Margaret for trying to ruin my life.

Perhaps Eddy was right. Maybe I did need to rethink my opinion of Tristan. Perhaps he wasn't as awful as he appeared. By the time we pulled into his driveway, I'd decided I owed him at least one chance to prove he wasn't so bad. I'd try to be friendly, even if he did dress weird and talk like a dolt. Eddy honked the horn a couple of times while the old truck rattled in neutral. We waited a bit, then she honked again.

"I guess he can't hear us," she said. "I'll go and knock on the door."

"That's okay, Eddy. I'll go." I jumped out of the truck and walked up to the front door. Even before I got there I could hear the TV blaring away inside — no wonder he couldn't hear the horn. I could see through the sheer curtains that someone was sitting on the sofa in front of the TV. I knocked, but there was no answer. So I tried again, pounding louder.

"Go away and stop bothering us," came a growly voice. "Can't you tell no one wants you here?" I couldn't make out if the voice was a man's or woman's, but I definitely got the point when the volume on the TV got louder.

"No one home?" Eddy asked when I got into the truck and slammed the door.

"Oh, there's someone home — just too busy watching that cliff-hanger reality show *Cooking with Pee Wee Herman* to answer the door."

"Well, it couldn't have been Tristan. If he'd been home, he would have answered the door."

"Would he now? So why isn't he home then? You said you'd come for him, right?"

"There must be an explanation," Eddy said quietly as she pondered the situation.

"Perhaps m'lady should consider that if Sir Tristan isn't home, as he said he'd be, it could mean the greasy Romeo is off pillaging yet another sacred historical monument." I watched as the space between Eddy's eyebrows disappeared and her mouth became a thin line. That was when I realized I'd really upset

76

her. For now it was best if I just buttoned up and sat quietly as we drove the short way to the site.

Eddy's problem was that she was just too nice. She wanted to trust and help this kid, but her professional reputation was on the line now. I knew I was right about this. Besides all of the signs and evidence against the guy, I had sharp personal instincts that told me Tristan wasn't to be trusted. I mean, hello, he'd been caught red-handed, he hid behind creepy dark clothes and thick black makeup, talked with a phony British accent, and spouted all that Shakespearean drivel that made no sense. Like it or not, he was a loser, and if I didn't help Eddy face facts, she was going to get hurt.

It took Eddy and me all morning to clear the brush around the burial. We also had to cut down two skinny saplings that were in the way and remove the clumps of grass and prickles. My arms and hands looked as if they'd been in a war and lost. What made it extra hard was working on a forty-five-degree slope with loose gravel underfoot. It was lunch by the time we finally managed to clear a rectangle the size of Aunt Norma's kitchen table. At least now it was easy to see the oval ring of stones outlining the convex mound that formed the burial.

The next major problem we had was setting up a three-legged screening station close to the burial. Even with all of Eddy's experience, we still had a hard time finding a way to keep the station steady on the slope. And rescue excavation or not — Eddy insisted it was to be as accurate and scientific as possible. Before we even touched the casket and skeletal remains we were going to have to clear the entire thing by digging up one bucket full of dirt at a time and sift it all through a screen just to make sure we hadn't missed any small artifacts. I knew that when we got to the coffin everything would have to gear down and out would come the trowels, soft-haired paintbrushes, and dental picks.

I wanted Eddy to test out her new subsurface radar scanner. I thought it would be a good time to see if it could really penetrate the ground and reveal if there were any human remains down there. But she said there wasn't any point, since she already knew there was a coffin below. Hey, she was the expert!

By 1:30, Eddy looked like a red puffer fish gasping for air on dry ground. But she had a schedule to keep, so we continued for another two hours. She wanted to keep working until the entire site was mapped and our datum points marked. That way we could measure the depth of the burial below the surface once we started digging.

I had to admit that it would have been a lot easier and quicker with another pair of hands. I guess that was something Eddy had known before we'd even begun. Maybe it was the real reason she had invited Tristan to help. Still, I would rather we struggled alone than have an irresponsible guy like him around.

"Let's take a break," Eddy suggested. "I'll drop you at your aunt's and I'm going back to Mary's Motel for a shower and nap. We can pick up another couple of hours of work before nightfall." The afternoon sun was shining full force on the hillside, and I was feeling a bit like melted wax.

When I returned to Aunt Norma's house, I wasn't surprised to find it empty. Then Licorice startled me again when he crawled out from under the coffee table where I guess he'd been curled up on a pile of newspapers. There was a note stuck on the fridge along with a guidebook of the town:

Hi, Pegs,

If you get home before me and are looking for something to do, why not make a trip to our little museum? It's open until 6:00. Say hi to Henry for me if you go.

XXOO
Aunt Norma

Since Eddy wasn't coming back for a couple of hours, I decided to take Aunt Norma's suggestion. I tucked the Golden guidebook under my arm and headed out the door. I knew Golden wasn't much bigger than Crescent Beach, the town where I lived, so it wouldn't take long to do a quick walk around and then visit the museum before it closed for the day.

Mom said there was a big difference in seeing a place from the seat of a car and walking its streets and lanes yourself. It was true. Maybe I had subconsciously seen the mountains surrounding the town, but I had never really looked closely at them. To the east they were steep, rugged, and covered in a thick hemlock forest. To the west stood a completely different range where each snow-capped peak rose like the Matterhorn at Disneyland and the blue-white glistening snow was almost too bright to gaze at. Behind every pointy mountaintop was the cornflower-blue sky. It all seemed like a postcard Mom and I had gotten once from friends visiting the Swiss Alps.

Even the fresh mountain air was somehow sweeter. I breathed it in deeply and happily walked down the road toward Kicking Horse River. The guidebook said that was where I'd find "the famous timber bridge — the longest pedestrian bridge in the world." Boy, someone must have wanted to put this town on the map awful bad to come up with that for a world record breaker.

I walked to the middle of the bridge and stopped to watch the muddy brown water churn beneath me. It was thundering past so fast and forcefully that I could feel the bridge shudder as I stood there watching it. And it was no comfort thinking how quickly a person could be swept along by its current with no way of stopping. They'd end up in the even bigger Columbia River in only a few minutes. That thought made my knees weak, and I was suddenly glad the world's longest pedestrian timber bridge had been built so solidly.

When I was little, my dad and I would walk down to the footbridge near our house. At the time that little creek seemed just as powerful to me as the Kicking Horse River. Dad and I used to play a silly game called Pooh Sticks that I'd learned from Winnie the Pooh on TV.

Just for fun I gingerly made my way down to the riverbank and collected three chunky sticks caught in the rocks. I returned to the middle of the timber bridge and dropped the first one into the rushing current, then dashed to the other side in time to watch it speed out from beneath me like a rocket and bob along on the surface of the water. When I could no longer see it in the distance, I crossed to the other side again and picked up the last two pieces. *This one's for me and the other is for you, Dad,* I said silently.

I dropped them both at the same time and again skipped across to the other side of the bridge to see which one would be the winner. It made me laugh as I watched my father's stick race out from under the bridge a split second before mine. For a moment I felt gloomy and wondered what my life would have been like if Dad hadn't died. Then I remembered Officer Hopkins saying that Tristan had lost his father, too. Two kids without fathers — one turned out pretty good and the other ... trouble.

After my game of Pooh Sticks, I strolled along Ninth Avenue and stopped in front of *The Golden*

Star newspaper office. I peered through the window and saw Aunt Norma sitting at her desk, talking on the phone. When she spotted me, she waved. I waved back and carried on past the old bookstore building and back across the Kicking Horse River on the Tenth Avenue Bridge.

By following the map, I eventually found myself at the gate of the Golden Museum. The building was an unimpressive corrugated metal tube — the kind some people used at the back of their acreage to store dusty old cars and parts, or bricks and lumber. But when I entered I found myself immediately staring at an eerie, surreal scene of the past — a mural of some white guy dressed in deerskin clothes with a couple of First Nations people by his side. And the black night sky was filled with stars that gave off an almost translucent glow that bathed the landscape. I could tell it was a picture of Golden because right behind the man were the same jagged, snow-covered peaks I'd just seen on my way to the museum.

"Fascinating, don't you think?"

I jumped at the voice and whirled to find a short old guy standing behind the counter. He wore a plaid shirt and a goofy old bow tie, and a little black bowler hat was perched on his silver hair.

"That's the great explorer David Thompson, and the Native guides who helped him discover the Northwest Passage over two hundred years ago."

I gazed at the mural again and almost felt it pulling me into the past.

"Welcome to Golden, young lady."

"Oh, thanks … can I come in?" I asked, still a little unnerved by the strange little man.

"May I come in?'" he replied, smiling.

"Sorry? Did you ask me something?" I wished I could hide my now cherry-red face.

"No, young lady. You were the one asking a question. By using the verb *can*, you were asking me if you had the ability or opportunity to come in to the museum, which of course you do. But if I understood you correctly, you were really asking me for permission to enter the museum. And if that was your intention, then the correct verb is *may*. As in, 'may I come in?' And, of course, the answer to that is, most certainly you may enter."

Okay, glad we got that out of the way. If the old guy's small round eyes weren't so bright and cheerful, I might have thought he was trying to make fun of me. But instead I made a mental note to add this little grammar lesson to Aunt Margaret's educational checklist. That ought to make her happy.

"Thank you." I moved a little farther into the main hall.

"It's so nice to see a young lady take interest in things of the past. We don't get many children coming here on their own. I suppose that's because there are so many distractions these days — TV, playing on the computer, going to the movies. May I ask, are you new to town or a visitor?"

I returned his smile. "Yes, you *may* ask. I'm a visitor from the coast."

He smiled approvingly. "So you're visiting? Well, isn't that nice? We don't get too many visitors this time of year, though this is really the best time. The temperature is quite reasonable, which means there aren't too many flies and mosquitoes, either. Makes it rather perfect, actually. We like to call this time of year our Indian summer. Would it be too bold to ask where you're staying?"

"No, that's okay. I'm staying with my aunt, Norma Johnson."

"Miss Johnson? Well, now, that's impressive. She's our town's best reporter — works over at *The Golden Star*. But of course you knew that already."

His eyes sort of twinkled when he smiled and made me think of Santa Claus if Santa were a real person and shaved. Of course, I didn't bring up the fact that Aunt Norma was the town's only reporter.

"My goodness! I just realized I haven't properly introduced myself. I'm Mr. Henry Murphy, but the young folks like to call me Uncle Henry. What's your name?"

"I'm Peggy Henderson."

Uncle Henry's eyes bugged out, and the pink buds on his cheeks grew like rosy apples. "Henderson? How wonderful! Could it be that you're a relation of the famous Hendersons?"

"Ah, I don't think so. I mean … who were the famous Hendersons?"

"Oh, dear, they were one of Golden's founding families. In fact, it was Mr. James Henderson who was responsible for designing most of the buildings in this town at the turn of the century."

"Is that the turn of the nineteenth century or twentieth?" I asked, knowing it was a cheeky question.

"That would be the nineteenth century, young lady," Mr. Murphy answered without hesitation. "Many of those first buildings are gone now, but if you know where to look, you'll find some of them are still standing."

I thought about the old newspaper office and wondered if it was one of the Henderson buildings.

Uncle Henry gazed at the ceiling. "Yes, the Hendersons. A fine bunch they were. Did you know they have their own private cemetery? No, of course, you didn't know that." He paused, then asked, "Will you be attending school while you're here?"

"Actually, I'm getting an education of a different kind, Mr. Murphy." I thought about what Mom had said to Aunt Margaret.

"Please, feel free to call me Uncle Henry. All the young people do. It's what everyone started calling me after I retired from teaching English and history over at the high school twenty years ago."

Well, that explained the little grammar lesson. "Okay, Uncle Henry, I'm here with Dr. McKay to excavate the disturbed burial over at the Pioneer Cemetery. Eddy's an archaeologist with the Provincial Archaeology Branch. When it was reported that a vandal had disturbed a burial, she was asked to come here and excavate it. I'm here to help her."

At first there seemed to be a moment of surprise on Uncle Henry's face, and just as suddenly the twinkle in his eyes seemed to fade. I figured for someone like him vandalizing historic sites was a real downer.

"It's too bad that archaeologist friend of yours had to come all this way. Wouldn't it be better to just leave the burial where it is?"

"Trust me. Archaeologists don't want to dig up everything from the past. They know that sometimes it's best to leave things where they are or at least leave some sites for future generations. But once a human burial like this has been disturbed it's got to be excavated properly before some careless gravedigger goes in there and destroys everything — like that kid who got caught was trying to do."

Now Uncle Henry really looked depressed. "Well, now, you didn't come to the museum to waste your time talking to an old schoolteacher like me. Please go on in and have a look around. Be sure to visit our schoolhouse and Golden's original train station, too. It was moved to this location years ago by the historical society."

"Where did they move it from?" I asked.

"It was on the other side of the tracks. In fact, right between the Pioneer Cemetery and the old town, to be exact. Well, enjoy yourself." Uncle Henry smiled one last time and disappeared into the office.

I had the feeling I'd be visiting the museum again, so I'd just take a peek at the old farm tools, hand-sewn leather clothes, and the small collection of

Native artifacts. What I really wanted to see was the old train station. Looking at it from the front, I found it easy to imagine the place as it was a hundred and thirty years ago when old black engines were gushing steam and tooting, and bearded miners passed in and out of its doors. There were probably pioneer families arriving, too — all bewildered, yet hopeful.

There were obviously some resident gophers whose heads popped up here and there from tunnels dotted around the grounds. They made an amusing sideshow. Their dodgy movements and little brown faces reminded me of a game I once played at the fair where I was supposed to hammer gophers with a large rubber bat as their heads momentarily popped out of the holes.

Will's head and broken ribs still ache from the pummelling he got the other night. When Colonel Spence notices he is black and blue and moving slowly, he asks the crew foreman about it.

"Must have been that runaway boulder," the foreman tells him. A day later Will gives the colonel the same answer.

Even though Doc told him to take a few days to let his ribs heal, Will refuses. He cannot afford to take time off. But even more important, he cannot risk losing his place on the crew. Then where would he be? No, it is better to work in pain than to risk losing his job.

The Golden Era
Golden, British Columbia,
Saturday, May 21, 1891, Ten Cents

MINERS STRIKE FOR BETTER PAY

Nine men from Silver City are out of work after attempting to incite a strike for increased pay. They were given their leave and within a matter of hours their jobs were filled from the pool of some fifty men hoping to get work at the mine. Let this be a warning to all working men, that greed is like a bottomless pit that cannot be filled. If indulged, it will result in misery and job loss.

TOO MUCH TIME ON THEIR HANDS

A Donald firm shipped fourteen hundred dozen empty beer bottles to Winnipeg. The mathematical editor of *Truth* estimates that to empty them caused three thousand three hundred and sixty men to imagine themselves capitalists, only to wake up with nary a cent and a splittingly bad headache.

CHAPTER SIX

"Hi, Pegs, your archaeologist friend called," Aunt Norma said when I came in the door. I was happy my aunt was home. "She says she'll be here at 6:00 to get you. She said something about getting in a couple of hours of work tonight. She's pretty ambitious."

"A regular workaholic, just like you, and the toughest grandma I've ever known."

"Well, I see you're in full admiration of her ... and me. But that only leaves you twenty minutes to eat, so how about some canned soup and crackers?"

"Sounds perfect." I sat at the kitchen table while Aunt Norma heated a can of gourmet cream of mushroom soup. "I took your suggestion and went to the Golden Museum. Met Uncle Henry, too."

"Good for you. Pretty neat little place, isn't it?"

"Yeah. I really liked the train station." A few minutes later Aunt Norma put down a steaming hot bowl in front of me. I blew on it and then fanned it with a *Golden Star* newspaper. "Uncle Henry didn't look too pleased after I mentioned I was helping Eddy excavate the burial in the Pioneer Cemetery."

"That's understandable. Henry's been taking care of all our important sites for decades. It hasn't been easy, either, with a town council that refuses to put any money aside for maintenance and repairs. You can imagine how Henry felt when our famous Sheriff Redgrave's headstone was found pushed over on its side and toilet paper was draped all over the ornate gate that had been sprayed orange."

Yeah, I could see how that would upset him. It upset me, too.

"Not long after that someone put graffiti all over Sergeant Ross's cross over at the Royal Canadian Legion Cemetery," Aunt Norma continued. "And to add salt to an open wound, the culprit left gaudy pink flamingos all over the grounds with little notes declaring that Sergeant Ross was a coward and a sissy."

"Eddy mentioned that something happened to the historical Swiss guides' homes, too," I said between mouthfuls of soup.

"Actually, nothing happened to the homes, but someone poisoned the trees that were in front of them. They all had to be cut down. Though I must admit, it's awfully nice to be able to see the homes in all their glory now from almost anywhere in Golden."

I gobbled down the last of my soup and drained a glass of milk.

Aunt Norma put down a plate of goodies. "There are a couple of other reasons Henry might have appeared upset when he heard about the excavation at the Pioneer Cemetery. I recall that he mentioned he has a distant family member buried there. I don't think it was anyone he knew, but with Henry family is family. Then there's Sam ..."

"Sure, who wouldn't be upset by that cretin?"

"No, you don't understand. You see, Sam has been like a grandson to Henry. They got very close over the last few years, particularly after the boy's father left."

So that was it! After treating the kid like family, like a grandson even, Henry felt betrayed by what Sam — Tristan — did. He must have been heartbroken when he found out. This new information only renewed my opinion that Tristan was a full-scale, prime A jerk and couldn't be trusted.

I took my dishes to the sink, placed them in the warm, sudsy water, and glanced out the window at Golden's snow-capped peaks. It was neat how they looked exactly the same way two hundred years ago when David Thompson first came here, and exactly the same ten thousand years before that when the First Nations people settled in the area. Those mountains were like a symbol that some things in life would never change. Mom was rock-solid like that, and Eddy, too. You could always count on them. But then there were people like Tristan. He was more like a mound of sand that shifted with every gust of wind.

I rubbed my stomach, which now felt like a balloon about to pop. I thought about undoing the button on my pants when I heard the familiar rattle of Eddy's truck out front. Stuffed as I was, I grabbed one more piece of my aunt's nutty banana loaf and rammed it into my mouth as I dashed out the door.

"See you later, Aunt Norma," I mumbled between chews. I was skipping toward the truck when I suddenly stopped dead in my tracks. There in the front seat sat Tristan, grinning ear to ear. Just as my arms flew up, Eddy beeped the horn and beckoned me feverishly. I felt like turning around and going back inside the house, but I remembered what Skip Hop-and-a-Jump had said. Somebody had to keep an eye on Tristan. And besides, after all my hard work, I wasn't going to let him be the first one to dig.

When I opened the truck door, Tristan tipped an invisible hat and then jumped over the seat into the back. "Hello, m'lady. Please make yourself comfortable in the front of the carriage."

I wasn't sure if I groaned out loud or not, but I made certain they both knew I wasn't falling for any of that phony politeness. Eddy shot me a quick little smile, which I took as her way of pleading with me to be nice to the kid.

"Yeah, hi yourself" was the best I could muster at that moment.

As I was about to ask Eddy why Son of Frankenstein had skipped out on us earlier, she whispered, "Perfectly good reason. We'll discuss it later."

Even though the sun was perched on top of the western mountain range, there was still plenty of light to work by. With all the vegetation cleared — no thanks to Tristan — we would now be able to get a lot done. I let down the tailgate and climbed onto the back of the truck to fish out the tools — a couple of pails, a dustpan, a trowel, a measuring tape, a plumb bob … stuff like that. An archaeological excavation was a scientific procedure, but it was funny how most of the tools to do the job could be found in an average garden shed.

"Ah, Peggy, I know you're eager to get started, but I thought I should teach Tristan about digging an archaeological site first."

Hot blood shot to my cheeks. "Oh, I think he probably knows plenty about digging already. Don't you?"

Eddy glared at me, but it was worth it just to see the smile on Tristan's face melt into an awkward grimace.

"Tristan, come with me. Peggy will man the screening station for now."

After looking forward to excavating that burial for days and then to be told to work the screen was like being sent out to right field after pitching a perfect game. I knew screening was important and all, but it was nothing compared to finding the artifacts in situ — where the old things had been in the ground since the time their owners had left them. And it didn't matter whether it was a piece of broken pottery or a stone tool or bones, there was nothing better than knowing at any moment I might uncover another clue to the past and become the first person to see, touch, and hold an object left behind hundreds or thousands of years ago.

While I stewed about it all, Eddy went through all the basics of excavating with Tristan. Like the right way to scrape dirt into the dustpan, how to spot an artifact, what to do when you find one, how to record its position and depth below the surface

— all stuff I already knew and was willing to do, if only Tristan was out of the way.

"The key to excavating is to use your eyes and to remember that your job is to carefully peel back one layer of history at a time just as if you were removing the layers of an onion," Eddy explained. "The moment you find something that might be of interest — an unusual rock, a bit of china, or even something that might look like nothing more than a turkey bone — put on the brakes and get Peggy or me. Once you fill a bucket, Peggy will take it to the screening station where she'll sift through the contents to see that no small artifacts were missed."

It took the graveyard genius nearly half an hour to fill the first pail and a quarter of the time for me to screen it. Every time he found something he'd get all excited and yell out, "Hail, hail, oh, queen" or "Friends, Romans, countrymen, lend me your ears!"

Eddy snorted every time and said things like, "Hold thy ground, oh, Marcus Antonius," or "Careful, oh, prince. All that glisters is not gold." Brother, I wished those two would lose the Shakespeare stuff and talk in a language I could understand.

In the first twenty minutes Tristan had called us over to see two pennies, a cigarette butt, and the tip of a ballpoint pen. Eddy gave me the job of explaining to him that pioneers wouldn't have had cigarettes with filters and that they were still using quill tips and not ballpoint pens. And as for the coins, I didn't need to say much after we cleaned them off and checked the dates — 1967 and 1975. All the same, Eddy made me show Tristan how to store all that junk and fill out a site level form for practice.

Archaeologists love to give sites friendly names, like when we found the remains of the old Coast Salish man in Aunt Margaret's backyard and Eddy named it Peggy's Pond. So I got Tristan to write Golden Pioneer Cemetery beside the site designation EhQf-16 on the line where it read "site name and number" and stuffed the form in with the level bag. Once the excavation was completed, all the artifacts and remains would be taken back to the lab where Eddy would be able to study them more carefully. Since every level bag held pieces to the big archaeological puzzle, it was really important that they didn't get mixed up. Only this particular bag would get a few chuckles, I'm sure.

When it was finally my turn to dig, I pulled up five buckets to every one of Tristan's. He was getting so far behind at the screening station that Eddy had to help him. I quietly snorted when I noticed the beads of sweat on his forehead. Despite the pleasure I was getting from showing Tristan up, knowing there was a coffin centimetres below probably had more to do with how fast I was working.

As the sun dissolved behind the Purcell Mountains, it got harder to keep the ten-centimetre levels even. I knew it wouldn't be long before Eddy would call it quits for the night. But thankfully just before packing it in a shape began to emerge in the soil — the distinct outline of a six-sided coffin. I knew the wood was dry and fragile — rotten even

— and I'd have to go carefully so as not to collapse the lid, crushing everything underneath it. I realized just how lucky it was that Tristan had been caught before he had done any real damage.

"We're almost there, Eddy," I said. "The casket and remains are just below."

"You're right, Peggy. That's definitely the lid of the coffin coming into view." Eddy used the tip of her boot to point to the tapered edges of the box. "Right now the first question that comes to mind is why the head of the coffin is facing west instead of east."

"What's so important about that?" I asked.

Tristan, who had been quiet for the past few minutes, suddenly piped up. "I think I know."

I felt like telling him I wasn't interested in what he thought he knew, but held my tongue.

"Uncle Henry told me that in the past if someone died before being baptized in the church he was buried facing west."

For the first time since I'd met him, Shakespeare Boy spoke normally and without the fake British accent. Then I remembered that the archaeology report mentioned other graves positioned like this one.

"He also said," Tristan continued, "that sometimes bad people were buried like this — with their heads to the east."

"That's an interesting bit of anthropological information, Tristan," Eddy said. "It's true. There were many early beliefs and superstitions regarding the direction or orientation of a burial. Many religions held the idea that if the deceased was buried with the head to the west, he would then be able to see the sun rise on Judgment Day, whenever that time might come, and be taken up into heaven. This belief probably evolved from ancient sun worshippers."

"Wait a minute," I said. "Let's go back a bit. If some guy was, let's say a criminal, in order to punish him after he was dead his body was buried so he'd never see the sun rise again?"

"Right," Eddy said. "Theoretically, it was so his soul would never get to heaven. Sad thought, isn't it?"

Sad? I thought it was flippin' terrific. Finally, something interesting that made me want to stop and scratch my brain. "So this might be the burial of some bad person — a swindler, a bank robber, or even a murderer!"

"Time is the justice that examines all offenders," Tristan mumbled, his head bowed.

"Hey, Dark Lord, for once just speak English!"

"It is English, you tempestuous maiden whose words are sharper than a serpent's tooth. But if you wish me to speak in simpleton terms ... Ultimately, no wrong deed goes unpunished, so there's no need for us to be this man's judge and jury."

"Okay, put down your sword, Duke Senior, and your dagger, Lady Rosalind," Eddy said. "At this point there's absolutely no reason at all to jump to ethnographic conclusions. We don't know yet if the direction of this burial means anything at all. Without closer examination or even written records, anything's possible and nothing is for sure."

"Written records?" I said. "Maybe there are. Wouldn't it be cool to find out this was some criminal and that he was buried like this because someone wanted to punish him for eternity? Right on, finally, a bad guy who got what he deserved." I looked at Tristan and batted my eyes.

"And why does the young lady so eagerly wish to embrace the notion that here lie the remains of a villain? It is more likely an ill-begotten premise. And as the good professor has stated, there are other possible reasons for the positioning of this burial."

"You think?" I chirped back. "I wonder what direction they would've buried you?"

Tristan turned quickly away. This time he was the one whose face was turning five shades of red. "The maiden's sharp words make it clear she does not suffer from a nature too full o' th' milk of human kindness."

I didn't actually understand what he'd said, but I knew it was an insult. "Look, Shakespeare Boy, archaeologists are interested in the small details. We're like detectives, and this here is a clue to knowing more about this guy. There's a reason this person was buried like this, and like it or not, one good possibility was that he was a criminal. And, yes, maybe even a murderer." That last bit gave me goosebumps.

"If this were play'd upon a stage now, I could condemn it as an improbable fiction."

Man, where does the guy get this stuff? I wondered. *Has he been living in the land of pretend his whole life?*

"Lord, what fools these mortals be!" Eddy said with an uncharacteristic edge in her voice. "Both of you stop! The role of the archaeologist is to consider the physical evidence. Theories for cultural behaviour can only be suggested after careful consideration of any available historical or ethnographic information. And without an eyewitness or specific written documents accompanying this burial, the best we can hope for is to make general statements and possible explanations."

Historical documents — that was it! If written information was what we needed, then Uncle Henry was the best person to help. The next chance I got I was going to make a visit to the museum to see if maybe he knew of some old records that named the people buried in the Pioneer Cemetery.

"Okay, that's it for tonight. Time to pack up." As if Eddy could tell what I was thinking, she added, "Peggy would love nothing better than to dig through the entire night, but I'm ready for a good night's sleep, and you two need to cool your heels."

After we dropped Tristan off at his house, I had the feeling I was going to get an earful from Eddy.

"Peggy, I have to say I'm really surprised by the way you've been behaving toward Tristan. Of all people, I thought you'd be the one to see the importance of giving him another chance."

The thought of Walter Grimbal, the man I locked horns with in my last adventure, flashed in my mind. Even after he made a career of selling ancient Native artifacts illegally, I believed he had it in him to change … and he did.

"But this is different," I said. "This guy betrayed his best friend, a man who treated him like a grandson. Henry Murphy trusted Tristan and was probably the one who showed him the location of the burials in the Pioneer Cemetery in the first place. Tristan must have known how important Golden's past is to Uncle Henry."

"I know it doesn't look good, but the boy needs our help. Even more important, Peggy, he needs your help."

She was probably hoping I would feel guilty. "Eddy, how can you trust someone who pretends to be someone else? He doesn't use his real name, he talks with a fake accent, and he uses stupid phrases from some guy who lived a million years ago."

"Actually, Shakespeare lived only four hundred and fifty years ago."

"So, okay, four hundred and fifty years ago. The point is he's phony."

"I agree his behaviour is odd, but did you think that maybe he's just trying to cover up how he really feels about himself?"

"Eddy, aren't you the least bit concerned that the kid might go back to the cemetery tonight and trash the burial and steal something important?"

"The thought has crossed my mind, but I'm willing to take the chance. That's because one time a spunky young girl taught me that sometimes we have to make a leap of faith and trust that most people really are good, even when sometimes they don't act like it."

That night I had a hard time falling asleep. Part of me wanted to agree with Eddy, but all the evidence pointed to the fact that Tristan was bad news. Somehow Eddy needed to see that ... for her own good.

I decided I'd browse through a book she gave me with the idea it might help make me drowsy. But instead *Burial Practices of the North American Pioneer* got my brain cells popping like a lightning storm. It talked about how a long time ago the first pope of the Catholic Church, Leo the Great, told his followers not to give a Christian burial to people who didn't measure up to his idea of a good person. That included anyone who didn't agree with the Church's rules, or had never been baptized, or belonged to a different race or religion. Other people who weren't allowed to have proper Christian burials were those considered to be notorious sinners, lunatics, those killed in a duel, those who took their own lives, and sometimes even children. Man, this guy was harsh.

Then I read how the Romans preferred cremation, but if they wanted to dishonour someone, they buried him. And if they wanted to be extra mean, the guy was buried face down. I also read that burying bodies with the head to the west and feet to the

east went as far back as the Iron Age. By the time
Europeans came to North America, a lot of the same
rules for burial applied.

All that reading only left me with questions, not
answers. Was the position of the burial out at the
Pioneer Cemetery random, or did it mean something? If it meant something, was it to punish or
humiliate? Or was the orientation just marking the
grave of someone never baptized. I could only think
of one way to find possible answers, and tomorrow
I would definitely visit the museum and get Uncle
Henry's help.

*The only light in the tunnel comes from the dim lamps
of the few men working alongside Will. In the few
moments of silence he can hear the sharp clink of axes
hitting rock as far away as tunnel nine.*

*Will is on chute pulling today — one of the deadli-
est of jobs. When big chunks of rock build up and bridge
across the chute, plugging the pipe, he must reach over
the boards and up into the empty space with a steel
pole to loosen the obstruction. He knows he must keep
his mind sharp and his lamp light fixed on the end of
the pole where it makes contact with the blocked rocks.
After he pokes the rocks hard and fast, he quickly pulls
his head back while tons of rock come crashing down.*

*It is in the middle of such a dangerous procedure
that he hears footsteps approaching and low, grum-
bling voices.*

"Maguire, you're to leave this and come with me!" barks the foreman. "Colonel Spence wants to see you."

Will puts down the chute pole as he is told and follows the bearded man back up the mine tunnel. When they arrive at the surface, Will's eyes squint until they adjust to the blinding brightness of daylight.

"What's this about?" Will asks nervously. Colonel Spence has never asked for him before. What could he possibly want to talk to Will about?

"Shut your gob," the foreman says gruffly. "You'll find out soon enough."

Will follows the man toward the back of the dining tent. A small group of men are standing around while Cook yells something about his life's savings. As Will approaches, he hears a familiar voice spewing venom.

"The Maguire kid did it — I just know it!" shouts Thomas Moody. "His father's a convicted murderer, so we all know crime runs in his blood." Colonel Spence, Moody, and the other men in the group turn and face Will. "That's him there. I'd bet my last dollar it was him that did it."

Will is not sure if his face is warm from shame or anger.

"What have you done with it, boy?" Cook demands. "Where have you stashed my money, you spineless thief?"

Will jumps back instinctively and raises his hands as the old man flails his chopping blade in the air.

"Control yourself, Cook!" commands Colonel Spence. "At the moment we're just questioning the boy." Colonel Spence turns to Will and looks at him with eyes that could penetrate steel. "William Maguire, *where were you between last midnight and this morning before breakfast?"*

Will almost laughs at the question, for there is only one place he can be found every night when the men are out drinking and womanizing in the saloon — he was in bed. Most often he is so dog-tired that he is half asleep before his head hits the pillow. Some nights he is unlucky and lies awake trying to fight off the memories of betraying his father or worrying about his mother. Those nights he would rather his body were racked with pain so he would have something else to think about.

"I was in my bunk sleeping, sir," Will answers, doing his best to hide the quaver in his voice.

"Liar!" accuses Moody. "You snuck into the kitchen when everyone else was in town and stole Cook's money, didn't you?"

"No! I never."

"Son, if you're lying and we find out you did it, you'll not only be sacked, but I will make sure no other mining company in British Columbia takes you on," says Colonel Spence. "But if you confess now and return Cook's money, you'll only be fired."

Will is shaking so much now there is no way of hiding if from the others. He wrings his sweaty hands. "I never did it, Colonel. I swear." Cook lunges at him again, only to be blocked by Moody.

"Look at him! It's obvious he did it. Anybody can see the boy's a liar and a thief by the sweat on his brow and the shake in his voice. All he needs is a swift cuff in the head to get him to talk — like this!" Moody brings his

fist down quickly to Will's shoulder, driving him to the ground and dislocating his arm.

As the boy cries out in pain and writhes on the ground, Cook's helper comes running out of the kitchen holding a small leather pouch. "Look! Look what I found in the barrel just as I was about to pour in the new bag of flour. Isn't this your purse, Cook?"

Cook snatches the wallet and quickly opens to check the contents. "Thank you Jesus, Joseph, and Mary — it's all here." He closes the purse and kisses it. "It must've fallen out of my pocket yesterday when I bent over the barrel to scrape the last of the flour for the supper biscuits."

All eyes now turn toward Will, then to Thomas Moody and Colonel Spence.

"Well, it seems everything has worked out fine. You men may go back to work. Foreman, you take Mr. Maguire to the medical tent to see about that arm of his." As everyone turns to leave, Colonel Spence interrupts. "Not you, Moody. You come with me."

Moody gives Will an evil glare as he follows the colonel away.

That evening, while his shoulder throbs, Will eats his supper in peace. It is the closest thing to happiness he has felt in years.

The Truth
Donald, British Columbia,
Saturday, November 21, 1891, Ten Cents

MINER ROBBED AND KILLED

This past week on the trail to Farwell, Arthur Tipper, a respected miner, was found shot to death. It was said he was in possession of $4,000 at the time he departed on foot from Donald. At the time of this printing no suspects had been apprehended. Although one witness claims he was seen in the company of a large bearded man. They appeared to be arguing. Anyone who may have information on this case is instructed to contact Sheriff Redgrave.

AFTER CHURCH SOCIAL

The latest fashion for some of Golden's young people is riding in democrats drawn by horses rented from Mr. Hamilton's livery stable. For some these horse-drawn jaunts are more a parade of fashion. These young men and women are like a flock of peacocks all dressed in brushed velvet bowlers and fox-fur-trimmed hats with ivory lace. Perhaps this fashion show is mere advertisement for Golden's apprentice millinery, Rosie Heywood, daughter to

Robert Heywood of Heywood's Hardware. It was noted that the young hat-maker sadly has no time for carriage rides of her own.

SIKHS IN GOLDEN

Trains are filling up with workers from India heading for the boom towns of British Columbia. Many of them have already made their home in our area and there is talk that these brown-skinned people plan to construct the first Sikh temple in North America right here in Golden by the year's end. The editor finds it hard to understand why these warm-weather birds would want to flock to the snow-packed Kootenay region. They would be better far from here, sunning themselves in their own country.

CHAPTER SEVEN

"Aren't we picking up the Dark Knight this morning?" I asked when Eddy drove past his house and directly on to the site.

"No."

No? Why not? What happened? That single word could mean anything — good or bad — yet it left me feeling as if I'd been rammed in the gut with a basketball. I was already picturing the mess — a smashed-in coffin lid, human remains chucked everywhere, valuable artifacts stolen. It would be a tragedy to find the burial ruined, for sure, but then I had tried to warn Eddy.

As my chest was heaving with self-justification and I was about to give Eddy the I-told-you-so speech, we arrived at the site to find Tristan sitting calmly next to the excavation pit. The protective tarp was neatly folded, and all the tools were laid out ready to use. Even the loose rocks that had slid down the hillside through the night were cleared, and a log had been placed in just the right way to hold back more scree from tumbling into the excavation pit. When I looked, I saw that Eddy was wearing one of her proud grandma smiles. That stung, mostly because I knew it wasn't for me.

"Greetings on this fine morn," Tristan spouted, then swooped his hand and bowed as if he imagined himself a gallant Prince Charming.

Oh, barf! But what was even worse, Eddy returned his bow with a curtsy.

"Now we go in content, to liberty ..." she chirped.

"'Tis true, oh, Celia ... 'tis true."

So that was how it was going to be. I knew Tristan was nothing more than a smooth-tongued snake, but he had Eddy wrapped around his finger. At that moment I imagined I was about as welcome as a piece of gum stuck to Eddy's heel. I slunk over to the screening station so Eddy and Romeo could gush in Shakespearean babble jabber.

"Peggy, where are you going?" Eddy asked. "I need you."

"Naw, you've got all the help you need." I reached up and tightened the cinch at the top of the screen.

"But it's time we unveiled our friend here."

"You mean take the lid off? Don't you want to clear the matrix around the coffin first?"

"In a perfect scenario, yes, but I don't have time. This morning's weather forecast says a low-pressure system is moving into the valley in a couple of days, bringing one heck of a storm with it."

"'Ah, the cloud-capped towers, the gorgeous palaces, the solemn temples, the great globe itself, yea, all which it inherit, shall dissolve ...'" Tristan murmured.

Eddy smiled. "Yes, Tristan, 'and like this insubstantial pageant faded, leave not a rack behind.' Fine words as spoken by Shakespeare in *The Tempest*."

"Act 4, scene 1," Tristan added.

"Okay, already," I snapped impatiently.

Eddy turned again to me. "Right, so Peggy, as I was saying, now that we've exposed the coffin, it would be devastating if the pit was filled with rain and debris. I can't risk it. We're going to need to open this casket today so I can see what we're dealing with. If necessary, I'm going to try to arrange for a crane to come in and lift it out before the storm hits. So, are you ready, Peggy?"

Up until then my mind had been burning like a furnace fuelled by resentment, jealousy, and suspicion. I'd forgotten about the real purpose of why I was there. So like a wet towel, my excitement doused the fire.

"Am I ready? Do dogs have fleas? Do pigs love mud? Do skunks …"

"I get it — you're ready."

Eddy ruffled my hair, and for the first time in a while I saw that look in her eyes, the one she'd just given Tristan, the one that always made me feel mushy and sweet, like brownies just out of the oven.

"Okay, this might be tricky. What I need you to do is lean over the edge, Peggy, and feel around for a latch or something. It's possible there isn't one. In that case see if the lid will open. But go slowly and be very careful. At this point we don't want to do anything that would cause damage to the casket."

I got onto my stomach, and like an oversized worm, I worked my way around the outside of the

burial, sliding my hand along, groping for something that might be a lock or fastener.

"There's some metal bits here. I think they're
hinges." I continued around to the other side, but
there was nothing except the dry, flat surface of the
coffin. When I gave the lid a gentle pull, it lifted
almost effortlessly as if it were nothing more than
cardboard. But at the same moment Tristan shrieked
like a screech owl. I was startled, lunged forward,
and slid headfirst into the casket.

"Oh, no, Peggy! Stay perfectly still. Don't move."

Is Eddy serious? I thought. *Don't move?* My cheek
was resting on some dead guy's mandible. I squinted,
clenched my teeth, and tried not to imagine what it
was that I was feeling with my hands.

"Tristan, help me lift her out," Eddy said.

While my nostrils filled with gritty hundred-year-
old dirt, I could feel someone grabbing the seat of
my pants. Then my butt lifted into the air as if it
were filled with helium.

"Good job, Tristan," Eddy said. "Let's put her
over here, away from the pit."

Once I'd been dropped onto the ground, I
quickly rubbed my face on the inside of my shirt,
then took a deep breath.

"You okay?" Eddy asked.

I nodded back, but that all-too-familiar prickly
hot feeling was spreading across my face faster than
melted butter. "What about the burial? Is it okay?"

"The wood was so weakened that one side of the
coffin has collapsed onto the remains."

I felt like a pot of water boiling over and glared at Tristan. He seemed oblivious to the fact that it was all his fault.

"Sorry, Eddy," I said.

"Ah, what is gone and what is past help should be past grief," said Tristan.

What a twit! It was all his fault, and he was acting as if it was no big deal.

I wiped my eyes and nose and got off the ground. "Right, whatever that meant."

"I am simply saying there is nothing that can be done about it now. It happened, so no point in pining over it."

"You don't understand. Because of you I've destroyed valuable information. I've changed things. Now everything is —"

Eddy placed a hand on my shoulder. "Okay, calm down. I agree with Tristan. What's done is done. Unfortunately, accidents happen." She turned to Tristan. "But from now on we'll need to be very careful. No loud or sudden movements, okay? Now let's get on with things and see what we've got here."

We stood on the edge of the pit and gazed into the coffin. While my fall had caused the brittle wood to splinter and cave in on the right side, it wasn't long before I found myself staring into empty eye sockets. They held my imagination so strongly that it was nearly impossible to pull away from their sightless gaze. It seemed like one of those optical illusions where the eyes in a painting follow you no matter where you move in the room. I could feel goosebumps spreading from head to toe. I glanced over at Tristan and wondered what he was thinking.

While Eddy got out her camera, the two of us stood like statues. Immediately, I noticed that the remains were completely different from the three-thousand-year-old First Nations man in Crescent Beach Eddy and I had excavated last summer. In that case the bones were yellowed and the skeleton was curled into a tight ball like a sleeping baby. But this one was different — both sad, and to use one of Aunt Margaret's expressions, creepy.

The skeleton was laid out straight. The exposed dry bones were white and dusty. The skull was cocked to the side at an awkward angle. The humeri, radii, and ulnae — all the arm bones — were folded over the chest, as in prayer. There were small patches of dried skin clinging to some of the bones. Curly tufts of auburn hair were still attached to the top of the skull. And the clothing was little more than patches of frayed black fabric eaten away by time and small creatures.

Questions leaped around in my head. Who was this? What happened? How did he die? From experience I knew it was only a matter of time and the bones would tell us more.

I looked at Tristan, who had stepped back and turned away. His face was pale and pasty. I figured it was a natural reaction for most people the first time they saw a real skeleton and wouldn't have been surprised if Tristan lost his breakfast. Instead of vomit pouring from his mouth, though, out came more

Shakespeare. "'For all our yesterdays have lighted fools the way to dusty death … out, out, brief candle! Life's but a walking shadow.'"

Eddy smiled sadly and nodded. Normally, I would have let out another groan or at the very least a raspberry, but I let this one slide.

In examining the timber casket I could see that it was brittle and bone-dry — no pun intended. And after a century of being in the ground, a lot of little critters had managed to claim much of the contents. The only other artifacts noticeable were several metal buttons scattered randomly between the rib cage and a bit of lace tucked under the skull. It looked as though it might have once been a small pillow.

"These rusty metal hinges were standard design — nothing fancy really. And it appears there was no lining in the casket at the time of burial, which could mean this was a hasty burial or the family wasn't able to afford a more lavish coffin." Using tweezers, Eddy gently lifted pieces of fabric.

"What are you looking for?" I asked.

"I thought maybe there would be more burial goods, like a small family Bible, a cross, or maybe a piece of jewellery. From my experience in dealing with historic burials, there was usually something of a personal nature."

That reminded me of the artifacts Eddy and I had discovered buried with the Coast Salish man in Aunt Margaret's backyard. There was a bone awl, a burin, and a hammer stone, as well as the delicate stone pendant. The people who had placed them with the body believed their loved one would need those things in the next life.

"Those would be the kind of things that might help in identifying a person, too, right?" I said.

"Yes, Peggy, Bibles were often signed by family members, and pieces of jewellery might bear the owner's initials or some other identifying mark," Eddy explained. She sat up and dusted off her clothes. "On the other hand, these bones speak volumes, too. Like the markings on the upper-right humerus were left by very large muscle attachments." She got on her knees again and practically stuck her head into the coffin.

"What's so important about that?" Eddy was really in a world of her own, and I didn't get an answer. "Eddy, I asked what was important about the markings on the upper arm."

"Oh, sorry. Large muscle attachments indicate this individual was engaged in very strenuous labour. Based on the history of this town, he must have been a railway worker or a miner."

"Or a farmer?"

"Yes, could have been. Whatever he did, it was definitely hard work."

"You keep saying *he*," Tristan said. "How can you tell it was a male?"

"Well, I can't say conclusively that this is a male until I've taken the remains back to the laboratory and done a proper analysis, including measurements of all the bones. But there are several indicators for determining gender, and just by doing a brief visual check I'm pretty certain this was a young man." Eddy picked up a narrow branch and used it as a pointer stick. "First, there's the pronounced supra-orbital ridge and squared mandible — characteristically, males had more pronounced eyebrows and chins, whereas females have flatter foreheads and pointier chins. The leg and arm bones appear to be longer and more massive than the typical female bones. And then there are these deep scars where the muscles were attached."

"I should think that women pioneers worked as hard as any man," Tristan said. "Wouldn't they have large muscle attachments, too?"

That was annoying — I was just about to say that.

"Good point, Tristan," Eddy said. "But there are still several other indicators that lead me to think this is a male. Like the external auditory meatus — the opening to the ear — is quite large, the pelvis appears narrow, the teeth large."

"How about the hair?" I asked. "Women in those days wore their hair long. This hair was definitely cut short."

"Touché, young maiden!" Tristan bleated.

Without thinking, my arm suddenly snapped out and I whacked him. "Cut it out with all that maiden stuff, will ya!" The second after I'd done it I was sorry. I was glad when Eddy filled the silence.

"Yes, the hair length is certainly another possible indicator that this was a male."

"You said he was young, Eddy. What about that?"

She pointed at some squiggly lines criss-crossing

the skull. "For starters, the cranial sutures are quite visible. You see, a young person's skull is made up of separate bones that don't finish growing until the late twenties. That's when they knit together and the sutures nearly disappear." Eddy stood and groaned heavily, muttering something about creaky knees. "Also, I can see that the epiphyse on the distal end of the right humerus didn't fuse. Another common sign in youths."

Eddy walked over to her pack and pulled out her camera. "I need to stop here and photograph the burial. After that I want to take some measurements and write up my notes. This might be a good time for you to take a break."

A break? I sure didn't want a break.

"You could walk back to town together and get yourselves some lunch," Eddy added.

"Nah, that's okay, Eddy," I quickly interjected. "I think I'll just sit over there under that tree for a while and make some notes of my own."

"Sign no more, ladies. I shall oft to yonder village and fetch us some victuals fit for a king, or rather a queen and princess." Then, quick as a wink, Tristan turned and headed down the hill at breakneck speed.

"Ah, there goes our gallant young prince, trouncing down the hill like a spirited horse, brave and true ..." I said in my best fake British accent. At first when I looked at Eddy her eyes were the size of golf balls and then the corners of her lips started to curl. At first it was just a little spluttering, but soon she was having an all-out snort and chuckle fest. She looked so hilarious that before long I was laughing, too.

"Trouncing?" Eddy said. More giggles mixed with snorts. "Where did you get that word?"

"Oh, you could say I've been boning up on my Shakespeare." I did one of Tristan's sweeping bows. "Actually, I think Tristan was glad to have a reason to get out of here. He looked a little green in the face to me."

The two of us passed the afternoon in near silence. It was a little strange that Tristan never came back. Eddy figured maybe I was right about him finding the sight of the burial too disturbing.

"Everyone reacts differently, Peggy. Now you, as I recall, were as happy as a pup that'd just dug up a stockpile of bones."

It was true. When Uncle Stuart and I discovered the ancient burial in his backyard, I found those human remains fascinating.

While Eddy worked, I made notes and diagrams of my own. When I looked up, I noticed she'd put little red arrows by three ribs and the left leg. "What are the arrows for, Eddy?"

"I observed that three of the ribs have calcium buildup, which suggests they were broken or cracked by a severe blow to the chest and then healed over time. And this deep slice in the upper femur, well, that's not so common. While these wounds weren't bad enough to cause death, they certainly suggest a dangerous life."

"Wait a minute. Did you say a slice in the femur? What would cause that?"

"Not sure," Eddy said, "but whatever it was it was sharp and driven with such force that it penetrated the flesh and then the bone."

"A knife?"

"Possibly."

I started to jot notes madly in my book: "Possibly a knife wound on left femur … broken ribs … signs of a violent life. Then there's the orientation of the burial. It might mean the people who buried him figured he was a pretty bad character — so bad they wanted him punished for eternity."

I glanced over at the brittle wooden box filled with those old broken bones and wondered about the day he was buried. Was there anyone there that day? Were the town's people glad to see him gone? Did anyone miss him? Was he really so bad?

At that moment I heard the crunching of dry ground coming from my right. When I quickly looked over, I spotted a small deer making its way up the hill. It stopped for a moment, and our eyes met. That was when I realized how peaceful that old abandoned cemetery was. There was nothing dangerous or foreboding about the place.

"It's your birthday?" Bennett Robson asks with surprise. "Well, doggone it, Will! Congratulations!" He gives his friend a happy slap on the back. "That sure

is a beautiful watch you got there from your mama."

Will holds up the gold pocket watch that came in the mail earlier. He fondles the decorative surface, wondering how much Mama must have gone without to get it for him. She even had the jeweller engrave a message and signed it "From Mother and Father." Will never imagined he would own a thing so fine.

"Hey, how about we celebrate by taking a trip to Donald?" Bennett asks. We could go tomorrow, Will. We could have ourselves a game o' pool, and supper at one of them restaurants. How about it?"

Will has never been farther than Farwell since he took the job at the mine. But then he never had a true friend like Bennett to go with, either.

"C'mon, Will, it's your birthday. A feller don't turn eighteen every day."

It is true. He is a man now and ought to mark the occasion somehow. Still, how could he waste money on himself, especially with Mama spending so much on this watch? He lifts it to his ear and thinks how beautiful the ticking sounds. No, he will be happy with his present. It is enough.

"Look, Will, besides it being your birthday, you've got something else to celebrate — no more Thomas Moody."

Colonel Spence fired Moody last week after he shot a poor Chinese man in the foot. Moody said it was because the Chinese man overcharged him for doing his laundry. Whatever the reason, Will is glad Moody is gone and has slept peacefully ever since. His spirits are so light that he finally gives in to his friend.

"All right, Bennett, I'll do it."

Bennett yips like a wild coyote, while Will tries to get his head around the idea that he and his friend are about to embark on an adventure. He hasn't been so light-hearted since before the trouble with Father.

It is Saturday morning, and the two young friends speed along the railway tracks on the 8:00 a.m. train from Farwell. Will has almost convinced himself not to be bothered that the return ticket cost him half a day's pay. When they arrive at the station in Donald, it is near one o'clock in the afternoon. As the train comes slowly to a halt, they spring onto the station platform like two light-footed deer. Full of joy, they continue to sprint along the road that leads to town. As they take the final turn in the bend, Bennett hollers at Will to stop.

"Hey, I just remembered. There's a meadow not more than ten minutes from here that's got lots of blueberries this time of year. Let's go fill our bellies before we go to town. That way we won't need to eat till later."

Will recalls Blueberry Meadow. He had gone there many times with Father when he was younger and they were making the trip on foot from Golden to Donald.

As the two friends jog along the path, Bennett chatters about his cousin, Lilly. "You'd like her a lot, Will. She's near sixteen years old, and people say she's the prettiest redhead this side of Dog Tooth Ridge. I suspect she'll want to get married soon ... when the right feller asks her, that is." He turns and winks at Will.

"*Don't think I'm going to be the marrying kind, Bennett.*" Will has never told Bennett that he gave his heart away a long time ago to Rosie Heywood. He used to write her but stopped when there were never any replies. For all he knows by now she has finally been married off to some rich man her father picked out for her. Mr. Heywood never liked Will, even before all that happened with Father.

"*Well, that ought to hold us over,*" says Bennett, patting his stomach filled with the sweet sun-warmed berries. He holds up his stained fingers, sticks out his purple tongue, and laughs. "*That's done saved us enough money that we can have ourselves some supper over at the Queen of the West later. Should be some pretty gal singing there on a Saturday. Then maybe we can head on over to the French Quarter afterward. I hear there's gonna be a dance later on.*" He slaps Will on the back and this time he howls like a wolf.

Will and Bennett make their way back along the path. In the distance they hear the sounds of Donald alive with activity — piano music, sudden bursts of gunshot, and much laughter. Happily patting his pocket, Will reminds himself to post the letter for Henry. His younger brother is nearly fourteen, and he is sending him a dollar bill for his birthday next month. He hopes Mama will let him keep it. With a sudden burst of energy, Will shoots passed his friend. "*C'mon, Bennett, we're missing all the fun.*"

The two race along the trail, each jostling the other to be in front. Finally, they explode onto the road and nearly bump into a man coming from town.

"Pardon us," says Bennett. In a flash they both realize who they have almost run into. Will all but faints dead on the spot as he looks at the huge man in black who is none other than a drunken Thomas Moody. Quickly, he steps back a few paces as a cold sweat washes over him. He stares into the man's icy blue eyes and hopes his shaking knees are not noticeable.

"Well, look what we have here. A couple of gaffers still wet behind the ears. Out for a bit of fun, are you? Maybe you've got two bits to share with a man in need? Eh, what do you say, boys?"

As the drunken Moody staggers back and forth, clutching his almost empty whiskey bottle, Will watches the expression on his face darken when he realizes who is standing before him.

"You! What are you doing out here, you snivelin' little Irishman?"

"Look, Mr. Moody, we aren't in for any squabbling," Bennett says. "We're just going to town for some fun. Now if you'll just let us pass ..."

"Shut your trap hole, you little sissy. My business ain't with you." Moody slowly slides his knife out from its sheath, and the afternoon sunlight glistens off the sharp blade. His deep laughter sends another chill over Will. "I didn't get a chance to leave my mark on you before the old man kicked me off the work crew. This'll be a little something for you and your pa to remember me by."

"I haven't done anything to you, Moody. Whatever quarrel you had with my father is nothing to do with me. You already broke my ribs and near tarnished my reputation. Isn't that enough vengeance for you?"

Moody's eyes burn bright with anger as he lunges forward. Will dodges the drunken man as he slices at the air. Moody whirls around and hurls the knife. The two stand momentarily facing each other, eyes locked together.

"Will, you've been stabbed!" Bennett calls out. "Are you okay?"

Suddenly, Will is confused. He glances down and sees the blade protruding from his leg. Almost immediately a steady stream of warm blood oozes along his pant leg. Without fully understanding what has happened, he turns to Bennett, then crumples to the ground.

A moment later Bennett is at his side, yelling at him to hold on, but he can feel himself slipping into unconsciousness. Bennett takes hold of the blade, yanks it out of Will's leg, and flings it into the bush. The shock of the action brings a brief moment of clarity, and Will screams with the pain. Instantly, his face is flushed and covered in sweat. Once again he feels as if his life is slipping away.

"You dog, Moody!" Bennett shouts. "Look what you've done." He turns to his friend. "Hang on, Will. You're gonna be all right. Just hang on." Bennett removes his bandana from his neck and ties it tightly around his friend's leg to stop the flow of blood.

"You say anything about this, Robson, and I'll come after you, too. You can count on that. Hear me?"

"I don't take to being threatened, old man," Bennett says.

Although Will is writhing in pain, he lifts his hand to Bennett's mouth. "Keep quiet, Bennett," he whispers. "Don't say another word."

"That's mighty wise advice," Moody snarls. "If I

were you, boy, I'd listen to him. Keep your nose out of our business and you'll be okay." The drunken man turns and slips into the woods.

That night after Doc Harvey has sewn up Will's leg the two friends rest quietly on the medical infirmary cots. Bennett is worn out from all the lying he has done to cover up how his friend got the leg wound. Doc thought it was impossible for a fall on a sharp branch while berry picking to cause such a serious gash. But for now he is not asking any more questions.

"I sure am sorry we didn't get to that dance tonight, Bennett," Will says.

"Yeah, me, too. Never mind. We'll get another chance some time."

Bennett is trying to sound cheerful, but Will knows he is still angry that Moody got away. Another few minutes pass, then Bennett sits up. "I know you don't want me to tell Sam Steele about what Moody done to you, but it's not right he be allowed to go around terrorizing people like that, Will."

"You're right, Bennett. But you don't know what Moody's capable of. He's got the devil in him and doesn't stop until he gets the upper hand."

"You got that right, and next time he's gonna try and kill you, Will. I can't just stand by and let that happen."

"If you let it alone, then things will calm down. You'll see. Promise me you'll keep your mouth shut about what happened today." Will waits, but his friend does not answer. "I mean it, Bennett. Promise me." Will sits up and stares at him.

"We'll see, Will. We'll see."

CHAPTER EIGHT

"Holy kadoodle!" Eddy yelped.

Her voice jarred me from my daydream, and my pen went flying out of my hand.

"This is exciting! I've never had one of these before."

I dropped my notebook and scrambled over to the edge of the pit where Eddy was lying on her stomach like a beached grey whale, gently examining the vertebrae attached below the skull. "What is it, Eddy?"

"These neck bones tell me this fellow suffered a sudden and violent hyperextension of the spine that caused axial loading damage. I'm sure it was the cause of his death. You see here? This disk and the second and third cervical vertebrae are crushed."

"Eddy, I didn't get a word you just said."

"Simply put, Peggy, this looks like a case of hangman's fracture." She was trying to get a rough measurement of the circumference of the cervical vertebrae with her calipers.

"Hangman's fracture? Just what are you saying?"

"I'm saying it appears this poor fellow was hanged to death."

For a nanosecond my mind blipped and then

flatlined. My hand instinctively clutched my throat and I couldn't help feeling creeped out by the news. "This guy was hanged to death?" I asked.

Eddy nodded and pulled out her notebook to write down some numbers.

I had to think about this. A hanging — that was extreme! But on the other hand it was pretty cool, too. Then I recalled our conversation days ago in the car on our way to Golden.

"You told me in the old days they only hanged people in Canada who'd been convicted of premeditated murder," I said.

Eddy nodded while scribbling more notes.

"So do you think that explains why this guy was buried with his head to the east instead of the other way around?"

"Could be."

"Oh, come on, don't give me that 'could be' stuff," I said with new energy. "All the details fit perfectly. It's got to be the reason, Eddy." I could hardly wait for Tristan to hear about this. I was due for some gloating.

"This has just raised the importance of this excavation a hundred percent, Peggy. I don't know of any other discoveries like this one. Nothing recent, anyway. I recall reading about a couple of cases found in old prison cemeteries that produced examples of hangman fractures, but I can't think of another case of hyperextension of the axial vertebrae in a public cemetery. This is the kind of discovery that comes once in a lifetime."

Eddy was as happy as a kid in a candy shop — a large pear-shaped kid — and her grin was so wide it looked as if her face was split in half. Unfortunately, her exciting discovery brought a sudden halt to our excavation.

"Sorry, Peggy, but for now we need to put everything away. I'm heading off to town to see what it's going to take to get a crane in here. Now that I know how important these remains are and that a storm is heading this way I can't take any chances. We're going to have to get this out of here as soon as possible."

I'd been looking forward to excavating this site myself bone by bone. So the idea that a massive machine was going to dig it up and then dump it onto a flatbed truck was about as welcome as the news from Mom that there was no Santa Claus.

As we bounced along the dirt road toward town, I remembered Uncle Henry. My aunt's guidebook said the Golden Museum was open until 5:00 p.m. on Saturdays. By my watch, it was just 2:30. That meant I could get there in time to get his help and do at least a couple of hours of research before the place closed for the day. Now that we knew this was a hanging victim it shouldn't be too hard to track down a name in an old newspaper or book. There couldn't be that many people in Golden who'd bitten the dust at the end of a rope.

Without telling Eddy where I was going, I got her to drop me off at the Tenth Avenue Bridge and took off at a sprint the rest of the way to the museum. I arrived out of breath ten minutes later.

Although my watch said 2:50, the doors were closed and locked. I banged a few times, hoping Henry or someone was still inside. But after pounding a couple of more times and getting no response, I sat on the grass, feeling like a flat tire out of air and going nowhere.

All I needed was a chance to get into the museum's archives. If I could do that, I might discover the identity of our mystery man, which would help to fill in a lot of blanks, not to mention make me hero of the day to Eddy. Just then I heard a noise coming from the back of the building. When I ran around to see what was going on, I discovered Uncle Henry climbing out of his car.

"Hey, Uncle Henry!"

"Samuel?" Uncle Henry looked up in surprise. "Oh, excuse me, Peggy. I thought you were someone else."

He had said "Samuel." Why was Uncle Henry thinking of Tristan? That made me wonder again why Goth Boy hadn't come back to the excavation site. Maybe he'd paid a visit to the museum already. If so, it meant Uncle Henry knew we'd opened the casket. I didn't know if that was important. One thing was for sure — neither of them knew anything about the hangman's fracture.

"Am I ever glad to see you," I told him. "I was worried the place was closed for the day, but now you're here. So can I come in?" I waited for Uncle Henry to correct my grammar, but instead he glanced around as if he was trying to remember what he'd been doing.

When he didn't bite, I asked, "I mean, may I come in?"

"What? Oh, yes, of course. Come in, Peggy."

"Where have you been?" I asked while he fiddled with his keys and unlocked the door.

"Well, ah, I had to take care of some personal business. I had to leave for a while. I'm sorry my absence caused you concern."

Uncle Henry was definitely off his game today.

"Was there something particular you were interested in, Peggy?"

"Well, actually, I was wondering if you know of some kind of list or record of people buried in the Pioneer Cemetery, particularly those who died of unnatural causes."

"Peggy, in those early days almost everyone died of unnatural causes. If it wasn't disease or starvation, it was some sort of accident."

Or maybe murder or execution, I thought.

"Unfortunately," he continued, "I don't believe there was ever a list of names for the Pioneer Cemetery. We know that the CPR used the cemetery as early as 1880. Then, later, miners and early pioneers were interred there, too, up until 1894 when the cemetery became too full and had to be closed. But no one kept an official record that I know of. The few names we have came from newspapers of the time, the occasional church records, and some unpublished interviews with settlers. When the last archaeological excavation was done, they discovered that Baby Douglas McNeill was buried there — he died at six months old. And

Robert Lane, too, who died at sixty-four and might just as well have been the oldest man in town at the time. And, I should add, the only one to die of so-called natural causes."

"Uncle Henry, is it possible you'd let me read the old newspapers you have in the museum archives?"

"Newspapers? Yes, I can let you do that." He opened the top drawer of his desk and pulled on some white gloves, then passed a pair to me. "The oil on our hands will accelerate the deterioration of these old documents, so please wear these gloves at all times when handling them."

I pulled the white gloves on. They were so long they went right up to my elbow.

"What year did you want to start with, Peggy?"

What year? I didn't have a clue, and I knew Eddy wouldn't want me to come right out and say *the year they had a hanging*. She wouldn't want information to go out to the public until she'd completed her examination and written her report. "Oh, I don't know. How far back does the paper go?"

"That depends. The first newspaper in the area was *The Truth*, started in 1888 in the town of Donald by John Houston. Donald's about twenty-five kilometres from here, maybe four hours' journey on foot. Then *The Golden Era* went to print in 1891. Of course, now they call it *The Golden Star*, the same paper your Aunt Norma writes for."

"I might as well start at the beginning. Can I look at *The Truth*, please? I mean, may I look at *The Truth*?"

Uncle Henry smiled.

A few minutes later I was sitting white-gloved at a large table. Man, those old newspapers were like trying to read a solid wall of ink. There wasn't much in the way of graphics or photos, or even white space. And half of it was advertisements — at least that was one part that hadn't changed much over the past hundred and thirty years.

With every page just full of stories, I decided the best way was to start by reading headlines: MAN DROWNS IN COLUMBIA RIVER, SHOOT-UP AT FORREST HOUSE SALOON, LOCOMOTIVE DERAILS EAST OF FARWELL, MAGUIRE TRIAL MOVED. The last headline definitely jumped off the page at me. I skimmed through the story that told how Kenneth Maguire was charged with murdering his neighbour, David Craig, over a dispute regarding water rights. It seemed the two met unexpectedly on the road to town. They fought, shots were fired, and Craig was killed. This article was just what I was hoping for. Now all I needed was to find later articles reporting that the court tried Kenneth Maguire for Craig's murder, that the jury found him guilty, and that the executioner hanged him. And, of course, something about him being buried in the Golden Pioneer Cemetery would tie it all up nicely. But how could I do that and not spill the beans?

"Hey, this is pretty rough stuff here about Kenneth Maguire. Sure makes for juicy reading. Got any more newspapers with articles about the case?"

Uncle Henry bowed his head and sighed. Then he brought the pot of tea he'd been making and two mugs to the table and sat across from me. "Yes, there are many more articles on that case, but wouldn't you rather I tell you the story?"

I nodded and held my breath.

"First," he said, "let's pour our tea, shall we?"

As I dropped four sugar cubes into my teacup, I had no idea that what I was about to hear would change everything.

"We'll go back to when my father, Henry Maguire, was nine years old. He had an older brother, William, and a younger sister, Emily. Their parents, Kenneth and Suzanna Maguire, had come out west with the building of the railway. Like many immigrants of the time, they dreamed of farming their own land. It was a hard life, harder than anything we could imagine. But they survived those first years with hope and determination. All that changed one spring when their neighbour, David Craig, a wealthy and powerful man, had the river that ran through their land diverted to his own property. It meant my grandparents' land couldn't support their cattle or crops anymore. They tried everything to get Craig to share the water, but nothing worked. After that it got harder and harder for them to make anything out of the farm. In practical terms it meant they could barely feed themselves. It was near the end of one very hard winter in 1888 when Grandfather unexpectedly met David Craig on the road to town. No one but him knows for sure what happened that day, but a jury convicted him of manslaughter. Some say he'd lost his mind and didn't know what he was doing. Some didn't think Grandfather was guilty at all, but were too afraid to speak up. Judge Matthew Begbie presided over the pretrial in Donald."

"Wow! He was the guy they called the hanging judge, right?" Man, I could hardly sit still. I was definitely onto something.

"Yes, but, in fact, Begbie sent very few men to the gallows. He was mostly known as a fair, respected, and, many would say, a man to be feared by all."

"So did he sentence your grandfather to hang?"

"No. Old Judge Begbie knew Grandfather would never get a fair trial around here, so he ordered the trial be moved to Kamloops. That's where there was a brand-new jail, courthouse, and gallows."

"Gallows? So then it was the judge in Kamloops who sentenced Grandfather Maguire to hang, right?" I was nearly ready to yank my hair out. When Uncle Henry raised his eyebrows, Aunt Margaret quickly came to mind. If she were here, she'd have cuffed the back of my head and told me not to ask such rude questions.

"Hang? No, Grandfather was never hanged. But he was sentenced to life in prison in New Westminster."

Nuts! My heart sank faster than a one-tonne anchor. Not because Uncle Henry's grandfather hadn't been hanged, though that would have made matters simpler. No, it just meant I had to do more digging around to discover the identity of the man in the burial. Then I remembered what Eddy had said about only premeditated murder being punished by execution. What a pea brain!

"It was a terrible thing to happen to a young family, Peggy. In those days, for a man to be sentenced to a life of imprisonment was worse than a death penalty — not only for him but for his family."

Uncle Henry handed me an old black-and-white photograph. It was brittle and cracked, but I could easily make out the five faces. The woman had a plain but kind look. On her lap sat a little girl with dark curls and an old-fashioned wool dress with a tiny bit of ribbon at the neck. And standing on each side of the stern-faced man were two boys. I guessed the smaller one was about seven or eight and the other could have been my age.

"That was my father," Uncle Henry said, pointing at the younger boy. "And the tall one was his brother, William."

"What happened after your grandfather was sent to jail?"

"Oh, it was a terrible time for the family. I guess you could say it was my Uncle William who saved them from ruin. At fourteen — only a year or so after this photograph was taken — he went to work in the silver mines and sent home every penny he ever made. Of course, it was a terrible burden for my father, too. At ten he became the man of the house and worked from sunrise to sunset on the farm. But he always said it was nothing compared to what William had to endure. Imagine, Peggy, William was a boy no older than Samuel, and he was off to work in the deep, dark mines with some of the meanest and rowdiest men imaginable."

"You know he likes to be called Tristan now," I said.

"Who likes to be called Tristan?"

"Samuel likes to be called Tristan, a knight of King Arthur's."

"Oh, that," Uncle Henry said, snickering. "Yes, that boy does have a vivid imagination."

More like a weird imagination! I thought. "Only Tristan's nothing like a Knight of the Round Table, is he? And I'm pretty sure he's not at all brave like your Uncle William, either."

"You say that because you don't really know Samuel. People have always misjudged that boy, Peggy. I realize there are times when he comes across ... well, let's say different. But that's probably my fault."

"Your fault? How?"

Uncle Henry laughed nervously. "I guess because I filled his head with too many stories. A bad habit for a retired history and English teacher, I'm afraid. Samuel loved learning about the Middle Ages and the legends of King Arthur. And then I introduced him to William Shakespeare. There was nothing he'd rather do than sit for hours and read and discuss Shakespeare's plays."

That explained the goofy way Tristan talked. "So he pretends to be something he's not by talking in Shakespeare quotes," I said, "calling himself a Knight of King Arthur's, dressing like —"

"Like the heart of darkness?"

I had maybe thought that but would never have said it quite like that out loud. "Yeah, I guess you could put it like that."

"I assure you that Samuel's not a bit like that. But to understand why he pretends to be someone other than himself, you need to know a bit about his background. His father abandoned him and his mother when he was eight. It destroyed his mother's confidence, and she took up drinking and watching television from morning till night. She gets a small welfare cheque — not enough really to keep them going. Samuel does his best to fill in by doing odd jobs or —" he hesitated for a moment "— stealing things from time to time. Mostly small things like apples from people's trees, or eggs from henhouses, or bread from the day-old rack outside the bakery."

I recalled the day I knocked on Tristan's door and saw someone slouched on the sofa watching TV. Thinking how I'd reacted at the time, I felt a numbing flutter of shame clutch my heart. "Didn't anyone notice he was just a kid who needed help?"

"He did a good job hiding the facts from most people. I noticed. And that's when I tried to find ways to help. But I would have lost his trust if I interfered in his life, so I just tried to be a friend. I'd bake too much casserole to finish alone, or would have a sudden dislike for canned vegetables. Hire him to do some odd jobs. I also started sharing my love of literature with him. Only I never imagined he'd immerse himself so deeply in Shakespeare's rich language or take on the name of a Knight of the Round Table. It was like it offered him an alternative to just being Samuel, the poor, unfortunate boy."

"And the black getup?"

"I'm not certain, but Samuel was deeply altered by Shakespeare's darkest of plays — *Macbeth*. The story is full of metaphors of good and evil. Tristan is the good knight. Samuel, who dresses in black, who breaks the law, is the evil one. It's not so illogical if you look at it from his point of view. People around here cast him as the villain long go, so he dresses the part. Only he's really nothing like that. He's a good boy, kind-hearted, and cares about —" Uncle Henry's voice got all wobbly, and he pulled out his handkerchief. "You know he's more at home here in the museum than anywhere else. He loves to sleep over there under the David Thompson mural. He says it's because he likes being reminded that the stars in his night sky are the very same ones the great explorer slept under two hundred years ago. I guess it's a comfort to him knowing that some things in life never change."

Huh? That's just what I like about stars, I thought. "I like that mural, too, Uncle Henry. But I'd much rather sleep at home in my own comfy bed."

"Yes, but in Samuel's case home isn't often a good place to be." Uncle Henry's eyes grew somber, and he got up abruptly from the table. "There are more of these old newspapers in the cupboard, Peggy. They're all in order, so help yourself. You'll have to excuse me. I have other things to attend to right now." He disappeared into a back room.

I couldn't say for sure, but the minute Tristan's name had come up it was as if Uncle Henry's mood had completely changed. No doubt he was upset. After everything he tried to do for Tristan, the kid repaid him by vandalizing historical sites, including nearly ruining a burial in the Pioneer Cemetery.

As sorry as I felt for Uncle Henry, I had other business to get on with, too. If Kenneth Maguire wasn't executed, then whose violently hyperextended neck bones were we excavating? I pulled out another *Truth* newspaper from the pile and started reading headlines: NEW MINE OPENS WEST OF DONALD, FUNERAL FOR THE LATE GENERAL SHERIDAN, DARING ROBBERY AT CAMPBELL'S DRY GOODS, MINERS STRIKE IT ON PERRY CREEK, TOWN WANTS A HOSPITAL — COMMITTEE FORMED, GOLDEN YOUTH CRUSHED BY TRAIN. I gulped. Now that was an awful way to go. It sounded like the kind of story Aunt Margaret wouldn't want me to read, but since she wasn't around …

Will abruptly awakens from a sound sleep befuddled by an unexplainable sense of doom. He wipes the sweat from his forehead and tries to shake the gloomy feeling from his mind. He reminds himself that he cannot afford to be late this morning.

As Will gently pulls the wool blanket back and places his feet on the cold wooden floor, he cannot help but wince. The wound on his leg still smarts. But pain or not, Will needs to get back to work. His family is counting on him. Will pulls on his dusty black overalls, grabs his lantern and lunch kit, and joins the stream of tired men stumbling toward the mess hall. He recalls that it is Thursday. Cook always makes cornbread on Thursdays — one of his favourites. Bennett's, too.

When he enters the room, the flurry of chatter he heard from outside shrinks to a few whispers. Will sets his lunch pail down at his usual seat, but can sense all eyes are on him. As he makes his way to the grub line, he feels a tap on the shoulder. When he turns, he sees Colonel Spence. The man has hardly even spoken to him since the day Cook's wallet went missing. Without the colonel saying a word, Will feels his breath catch inside his lungs and his pulse speed up like a runaway horse's.

"William ... something's happened ..." Colonel Spence pauses, then throws his arms up at the men hovering like a flock of scrounging crows. "What are you all looking at? Eat your breakfast and get off to work." He turns back to Will and clears his throat. "It's about your friend, son. I'm sorry to have to tell you that Bennett Robson was killed last night."

Will doesn't seem to be able to breathe, and his eyes are locked on the lines and creases worn into the colonel's face. "In the mines?" he asks mindlessly.

"No, son. He was found crushed to death between two rail cars outside of Donald. Somehow the release was triggered on one car, and it careened into the tail end of the other. For some reason Bennett was passing between them at the same time. I don't have an explanation for what the boy was doing there in the first place, but I can tell you that the accident happened so fast that he died instantly. Doc said his back snapped like a twig."

Will's head is in a fog, and he accepts the colonel's suggestion to take a little longer to eat breakfast before beginning his shift in the C mine. The other men slowly slip away to their work, leaving him alone in the mess tent. As he chews on his cornbread, he notices it has little flavour this morning. Even the coffee that normally sets his teeth on edge has no taste. Will is numb from head to toe, and the pain from the wound on his leg is barely noticeable now.

As he stares across the empty room, images flood his mind about the last conversation he had with his friend. They were arguing again over Thomas Moody. Bennett wanted Will to go to the colonel about the matter. He said it was bad enough that Will had lost a week's wages because of the stabbing. But it was another matter when he was forced to cover the medical expenses after his leg turned black and Doc had to come. But Will refused to tell because he was afraid it would make things worse for him.

"Doggone it, Will," Bennett said just the day before. "If you won't do something about it, then I will."

Will did not believe his friend would really do anything. Neither did he think anything was unusual when he didn't see him after his shift in the mine last night. They sometimes finished at different times, and both of them often fell into bed too tired even to speak.

Then Will's fist clenches into a tight ball, and without warning a volcano erupts inside him.

"You went there to set him straight, didn't you, Bennett?"

With no one else in the mess hall, Cook wonders who the boy is shouting at.

"I told you to let it go. I told you to stay away from Thomas Moody, that sinister, cold-hearted devil. But you didn't believe me when I told you he was dangerous, did you, Bennett?" Will pounds his fist on the table. "Now I have to finish what you started, don't I? I can't just let your death be in vain, Bennett. So now I'm going after him and I'll make him pay. I swear I'll make him pay." Will slams down his coffee mug, and like a storm, whirls out the door.

Cook stares after him, eyes the size of saucers.

Gently, I refolded the old newspaper and tucked it back into the pile. I felt sorry for Bennett Robson, even though I didn't know him. Being killed in a rail car accident was a horrible thing to happen to anyone. Uncle Henry was right — those were hard times and not many people got to live a long life.

For some reason I had a niggling thought at the back of my mind. I couldn't think why. Was it something I'd read? Something I'd seen? What was it? Then I knew. I remembered reading in the archaeology report a mention of one burial — I think it was burial fifteen — where the individual had four crushed lower vertebrae. In other words, a severely broken back. The Bennett Robson mentioned in the newspaper had to be the same guy that was excavated from the Golden Pioneer

Cemetery twenty years ago. I almost airlifted off the chair. Somebody ought to make me a detective! Then, like a penny dropping into a piggy bank, another idea came to mind. I wondered if Bennett knew the guy we were excavating. Hey, maybe they were even friends!

I walked into the other room to tell Uncle Henry the news, but I overheard him having what sounded like a very serious conversation on the phone.

"No, I don't believe he had anything to do with that ... Foster care? He'll only run away ... I can assure you he is not a menace to society. I can help him. Give me a chance."

It didn't sound like a good time to bother Uncle Henry, so I left the museum and headed home. I was anxious to find out what the news was from Eddy.

On the way back to Aunt Norma's, I stopped in at the grocer's on Tenth Avenue and bought myself a rainbow Popsicle. I was tearing off the wrapper when I noticed a familiar face smirking at me from his patrol car.

"Rainbow Popsicles — that brings back fond memories of my own boyhood in Kingston, Ontario," said Constable Hopkins, stepping out of his car.

He wasn't wearing his fancy red RCMP jacket or his wide-brimmed hat. I figured he didn't have time for "courting" today.

"I'd enjoy a bite of that, only people don't take police officers seriously when their tongues are purple." He snickered as though he'd said something funny.

A regular Jim Carrey! "Okay … well, see ya." I walked past quickly, hoping to avoid any further conversation.

"What's your hurry? You didn't rob a bank, did you?" He slapped his leg and hee-hawed some more. "As a matter of fact, I've been looking all over town for you. I wanted to find out if you have anything to report on our —" he stopped and looked around with shifty eyes to see if anyone was near enough to hear him "— suspect."

Oh, brother, not that! What was I supposed to tell him? I mean, Tristan was like having a burr stuck inside my shoe, but other than that and failing to bring back those "victuals fit for a queen," he hadn't done anything criminal — not that I knew of, anyway. But I was tired and gave Skippy the short version.

"Sorry, I haven't seen him do anything wrong, Officer Skip Hop-and-a-Jump." *Eek*, did I really say that out loud? Yup, the look on his face confirmed it. Man, I really was tired. I wondered if my face had turned a deeper shade of red than his. "Sorry, that just slipped out. I meant to say, Officer Hopkins." That did nothing in the least to smooth Skippy's feathers. But after he cleared his throat a couple of times and his face returned to its normal colour, I felt sure he wasn't going to shoot me.

"Never mind," he said sternly. He had on one of those clenched-teeth smiles. "I'm sure it wasn't your fault. You're bound to be influenced when forced to associate with a boy like Samuel McLeod. I'll even wager he was the one who made up that ridiculous name."

I wondered what Aunt Norma would do to me if I told him she was the one who had come up with that nickname.

"Well, no matter," Skippy continued. "His time has run out. I heard just an hour ago that his mother moved to Calgary and left him behind. And we certainly can't have a morally vacuous child running around Golden. Something's got to be done with him. It won't be too difficult to have him placed in a home far from here."

This must have been what Uncle Henry was talking about on the phone. Geez, Tristan's mother moved and left him behind? Although I wasn't crazy about the kid, I wouldn't wish something like that on my worst enemy.

"When's the last time you saw the boy?" Hoppy asked. "Do you have any idea where he's gone?"

I shook my head and mumbled something about not having a clue, which of course was true. Then I was suddenly aware I'd lost my appetite for eating a Popsicle and dumped it in the garbage. As I wandered home, I thought about how tough Tristan's life had already been — and now his mom had abandoned him, too. If he hadn't already gone off the deep end, then this would do it.

That evening Aunt Norma stayed home. It was the first night we actually spent having supper together since I'd arrived in Golden.

"I talked to your mom and Margie today. They wanted to know how you were doing. Of course, your Aunt Margaret asked if you'd been keeping up with the homework. I told her of course you were." She paused. "You have been, right?"

"Sure, I've been getting history lessons every day, grammar, too, and right now I'm doing research for the historical report I'm writing on Golden pioneers." It was true that I was learning lots of stuff, though I doubted Aunt Margaret would think any of it counted as "school work."

"You're looking a little glum, Peggy. Feeling homesick?"

What Aunt Norma took for glumness was really a big dose of guilt. I recalled the time when Mom moved to Toronto to find work and left me with Aunt Margaret and Uncle Stuart. As bad as it was being left behind, it was like a vacation in Disneyland compared to what Tristan was going through. And what really stank was how from the moment I'd met the kid I'd done nothing but call him names and try to get him into more trouble than he already was in. Okay, it was wrong for him to vandalize the burial and other historical sites, but Eddy was right. He needed my help, not my ridicule. *Please, somebody find me a rock to crawl under.*

"Would it cheer you up if I said tomorrow it's just you and me all day long?" Aunt Norma asked. "My slate's clear and I thought maybe you'd like to do some sightseeing, like visit the Northern Lights Wolf Sanctuary. Or we could go up to the ski resort. There's a neat little lake up there."

As awful as I felt, I perked up when I remembered there was one place I really wanted to see. "If Eddy doesn't need my help tomorrow, how would you feel about taking me to the Golden Municipal Cemetery, the one they've been using since the Pioneer Cemetery closed?"

Aunt Norma's mouth dropped open, but then suddenly she exploded into the biggest cackle and snort fest I'd ever seen. "Why should that surprise me, Peggy?" she asked after calming down a bit. "Honestly, you're the oddest girl I know and the only one who'd want to do something like that."

"What?" I protested. "There are a lot of things to learn in a cemetery. We could think of it as a history field trip." I was serious, but Aunt Norma just held her belly and laughed until her face turned red.

CHAPTER NINE

I let myself sleep in until almost noon the next day after a late call from Eddy the night before. She hadn't found anyone in town with a crane that could dig up the burial before Tuesday, so she was going to spend part of Sunday making calls to contractors in other towns like Kamloops and Revelstoke. When I finally stumbled out to the kitchen, I found Aunt Norma cooking up a storm.

"Brunch!" she said, beaming. "It's my specialty."

I started with a mug of hot chocolate and tiny marshmallows, some fruit salad, and little quiche tarts, followed by a delicious egg omelette ranchero-style and two slices of hot apple strudel topped with ice cream. I rolled off the chair and waddled to the sofa where Licorice was sprawled in the middle. He gave me an evil glare as I shoved him from his spot.

"Sorry, buddy, but you've got to learn to share."

He narrowed his eyes and then jumped off the sofa, tail flicking back and forth faster than a metronome keeping beat to the cha-cha.

That afternoon, as we drove through town, the low-lying cumulonimbus clouds were churning and rumbling above, threatening to ruin our outing. When we arrived, the cemetery parking lot was empty — big surprise, right! A cemetery wasn't exactly the kind of place that would normally be buzzing with activity. On the other hand, the dark storm clouds and wind whistling through the trees was a real bone-chiller to anyone who might be looking for that spooky graveyard atmosphere.

"Man, this place is dead," I said. "Besides you and me, I don't think there's another living soul around."

"Ha-ha! Peggy, you're one strange kid." Aunt Norma stuck her fingers in my ribs until I squirmed like a three-year-old and laughed until I could hardly breathe.

I know it might seem strange that a kid my age would want to go poking around a graveyard, but to me it was like an outdoor museum. You could say it was a chance to study history from a different angle. Headstones and grave markers were like small windows into the lives of people who lived in the past: "Here lies Frank Peterson — a good father and friend and a man who always kept his word." Of course, stuff like that always got me thinking about the families, too, like how they stood by their loved ones' graves the day they were buried and said their last tearful goodbyes. Okay, maybe that was kind of a weird thing for a kid to do.

At first the Golden Municipal Cemetery appeared to be a single, large, open space with neat rows of small plaques embedded in the grass. Some of the stones had small bouquets of dried flowers placed on top; others were nearly grown over with grass and moss. After a quick scan, I found that most burials were all facing east, even though they weren't that old. I thought of what Tristan had said about how some people believed it was important for the deceased to be able to see the sun rise "on Judgment Day."

Out of one eye, I caught sight of a gopher diving into a hole near one of the graves. They were probably the same little critters that had eaten through the coffin at the Pioneer Cemetery and chewed up the clothing and fabric. They were probably stealing it to line their nests.

As we wandered along, Aunt Norma called for my attention and pointed down the hill. "If you're interested in historical figures, you'll have to head down there."

I looked down the hill toward a little forest of hemlocks that had grown up between many weathered and grey headstones.

"The farther down the hill you go, the older they get," Aunt Norma added.

Just like the Pioneer Cemetery, I thought. "Eddy told me that hillsides were the best places for burying people back in the old days because pioneers couldn't afford to use flat farmland they'd cleared by hand."

"That makes sense. Did she also tell you this cemetery dates back to 1894?"

"Yeah, the same year the Pioneer Cemetery closed." As we wandered into the old part of the cemetery, I noticed how many of the headstones were surrounded by individual picket fences and that just like the others they faced east. I wondered if this was how the Pioneer Cemetery had appeared before it was abandoned and left to nature. Then I remembered there were no headstones, only wooden crosses.

As we walked along, the trees creaked and groaned above, while on the ground a thick carpet of dead leaves and needles crunched with every footstep. It would have been the picture-perfect scene from a late-night horror movie where the girl got nabbed by a pale scaly zombie. I quickly scolded myself for letting my imagination nearly run away with me. There wasn't anything to be afraid of here, right?

The farther down the hill we went the more overgrown and shabby the headstones became and the older the dates. The oldest ones were surrounded by stubby-sized Saskatoon shrubs and were overgrown with orange and grey lichen. Some headstones even had trees growing in competition for the same spot and were slowly pushing them from their place in the ground. I tried reading the words carved into them, but many were so weather-worn they were barely legible.

"Ah, here he is!" Aunt Norma crowed.

"Here who is?" I asked as I wandered up to the single headstone surrounded by a large and fancy silver fence. Compared to all the others, it seemed out of place. The entire burial had been freshly weeded, and the stone stood perfectly erect with fresh flowers placed at the base of it. I read the engraved name on the stone out loud. "Sheriff Stephen Redgrave."

"That's right — Golden's most famous and loved law enforcer. People say he was so respected that he often handed the keys to the jail over to offenders and told them to go and lock themselves in."

"And they did?"

"Usually. Though there was one guy who instead stole the sheriff's watch and some other things and then took off into the woods. But after a night of being nearly eaten alive by blackflies and mosquitoes, he turned himself in the next morning. He swore 'those critters were working for Sheriff Redgrave.'"

"Hey, wasn't this supposed to be one of the historical burial sites that were vandalized?" I asked. "The headstone says he died in 1903, yet it looks like the sheriff was buried yesterday."

"Yes, it was vandalized. Someone pushed the headstone down and spray-painted the fence pink. I wrote a story about it for *The Golden Star* and included a historical piece about the sheriff's life and career. Henry Murphy provided all the historical information. It got so much attention that the town council had to come up with the funds to have it restored. Then a group came out and added these flowers and held a memorial service. In fact, Skip Hopkins was head of the restoration volunteers. He said it was his duty to honour a fallen fellow law enforcer."

"Fallen fellow law enforcer? The guy died over a hundred years ago." It sounded as if the old Skipperoo was stretching the "fellow officer" connection a bit far. Maybe the guy was a history buff and all, but he was also a cornball to the nth degree.

"I guess you could say this was one time when vandalism paid off," I said.

"Yes, I guess it was. Prior to it, hardly anyone even knew who Sheriff Redgrave was or what he meant to this town. The headstone was tilting so badly it was only a matter of time before it fell over. The metal fence was rusty and broken. And the burial mound was overgrown with weeds and moss. Then it got vandalized ... and now it looks like new."

Hmm, that got me thinking. "You could say it almost looks better than new," I added.

Aunt Norma nodded.

"I remember you said the other historic burial that was vandalized was over at the Royal Canadian Legion Cemetery. Can we go there, too?"

"I suppose ... as long as the weather holds out," Aunt Norma said.

The Legion Cemetery wasn't far, and when we got there, it was just as dead as the other place. Okay, enough with the puns already. Being in a military cemetery, the rows of white crosses reminded me of soldiers standing at attention, waiting for inspection.

"Sergeant William Ross was a North-West Mounted Police Officer, right?" I asked.

"That's right. He worked under Sam Steele. They were assigned to police the building of the railway and bring law and order to tent cities like Golden that were overrun by rowdy, violent, and drunken men. I don't imagine it was an easy task, but eventually they managed to do it."

"So how'd he die — in a gunfight?"

Aunt Norma snorted. "Sorry, Peggy, nothing as dramatic as that, I'm afraid. No, Sergeant Ross died on January 1, 1885, at the age of twenty-four. Story goes he froze to death after breaking through the ice far from camp. By the time his rider-less horse returned to the compound and alerted the other men, it was too late for Ross."

It wasn't hard to find the sergeant's cross. It was the one that was so white that it almost gleamed and had a shiny gold chain surrounding it. And the metal plate with Ross's name engraved on it was polished to an eye-blinding shine. I couldn't see any signs of damage anywhere. Instead, just like Sheriff Redgrave's burial, it looked better than new.

"This is interesting, Peggy. There didn't use to be a fancy chain around Ross's burial place before." Aunt Norma scratched her chin and was deep in thought. "It certainly makes the grave look distinguished and raises its visibility as a historical landmark."

"Let me guess. Officer Hopkins led the volunteers in the restoration of this grave, too."

Aunt Norma nodded and her cheeks flushed.

"So what's the story?" I asked. "You said someone painted graffiti on the cross."

"Yes, and left pink flamingos stuck in the ground around it, too. But fortunately, the vandal used a water-soluble paint and it washed off." Aunt Norma stopped and glanced at me. "That sounds sort of strange, doesn't it? I mean, what kind of a vandal uses paint that —"

"Washes off," I said, finishing her sentence. "So in one case we have washable paint and pink flamingos, and in the other we have a knocked-over headstone that was about to fall down on its own. Instead of damaging them, the vandalism actually resulted in improving the condition of these burials and brought renewed attention to these historical figures."

"Exactly."

"And I seem to recall you saying that in the end it was a benefit that the trees in front of the Swiss homes had been poisoned and then cut down. You said now those historical houses can be seen and appreciated from nearly anywhere in Golden, right?" Almost on cue the sky began to rumble, and seconds later it lit up with fireworks.

"C'mon, Peggy, it's time to get out of here."

Before we even reached the car I was drenched. After that Aunt Norma and I drove home in silence, both deep in thought. All the fuss over what appeared to be vandalism to historical sites actually had the net benefit of improving them. But how did the Pioneer Cemetery fit into that scenario? Sheriff Redgrave and Sergeant Ross were thought of as heroes, but the burial at the Pioneer Cemetery held the remains of a criminal. That didn't make sense. What else didn't make sense was Tristan vandalizing the historical sites in the first place. From the impression I had gotten from Uncle Henry, he really valued things of the past. So why would he damage them?

As we rounded the corner, Eddy's old pickup truck was backing out of my aunt's driveway.

"Oh, Peggy, I'm glad I caught you. I really need your help." She was soaking wet, and I could tell by the deep creases in her forehead that she was worried about something. "The weather forecast says the winds are going to pick up tonight, maybe as much as two hundred kilometres per hour, and there's to be enough rain to float Noah's Ark." Just then a large branch cracked off from the tree across the street, and the wind blew it onto the neighbour's porch. "I wasn't able to get anyone to come and help us take out the burial. The best we can do now is to try to protect it from being damaged by the storm."

"What's the worst that could happen, Eddy?" I asked.

"Possibly a mud slide that will wash the entire thing away, or maybe trees falling on top of it. Either way the remains will be crushed, and that would definitely compromise their scientific significance."

After I grabbed my raincoat and put on boots, I ran back out to Eddy, who was in her truck listening to the weather report on the radio.

"So no luck getting a crane?" I asked.

"Actually, I decided against it. The only possibility was getting a backhoe. While it could remove the matrix surrounding the coffin faster than we could by hand, it would mean a lot of shifting of the ground. That, coupled with the slippery slope we'd be working on, it was bound to cause a lot of damage."

"It might not be a perfect plan, but at least we'd get the coffin and remains out before the storm causes them damage."

"True, but there's the added likelihood of destroying other nearby burials, and I just couldn't risk that."

"Other burials? How do you know there are other burials?"

"I went back last night with the subsurface radar scanner. Please don't look so disappointed, Peggy. I know you wanted to see how it worked, but I had to find out what the risks were before hiring the backhoe."

"So there are more burials? Where?"

"For starters the scanner picked up images of skeletal remains a few feet up the hill from the one we're currently excavating."

My eyes felt as if they were going to pop off my face.

"So you see," Eddy said, "I've had to make a difficult choice. And in the end I decided against pulling up this burial so not to risk interfering with the other one."

By the time we got to the cemetery, the wind had already ripped the tarp off the burial, and some earth and debris had started falling into the coffin.

"We'll have to leave that for now!" Eddy yelled into the wind. "What we've got to do is put the tarp over the coffin and fill the hole with that hay I brought in the back of the truck. After that we'll put another tarp over top and pile on as many rocks as we can find and hope for the best."

"Your plan sounds like the time my mom tried packaging an antique glass vase inside one of those bubble pack envelopes and mailed it to a friend."

"How did it make out?" Eddy asked.

I shook my head. "Not good, I'm afraid."

The light faded quickly and the wind and rain picked up, making the work ten times harder. It was the first time I actually wished we had Tristan's help. When we finally secured the burial, Eddy drove me back to Aunt Norma's house.

"Have you seen Tristan?" I asked cautiously as we pulled into the driveway.

"No. And it's been concerning me. That annoying police officer was by asking questions about him and told me about his family situation. Poor boy."

When I got inside the house, I was too physically and emotionally exhausted to do anything more than flop onto my bed. Even Aunt Norma's shepherd's pie and chocolate cake couldn't get me up. I stared out the window where the wind and rain seemed to be pounding the life out of everything. But the storm outside wasn't the only force trying to ruin everything and turn my adventure into one of Shakespeare's tragedies.

"I tell you, as sure as the devil has horns, that boy has lost control of his faculties," Cook tells Colonel Spence while a small assembly of miners stand by listening. Enjoying the attention, he takes a long pause before continuing. "I heard him talking to the dead boy and telling him a thing or two. Then all of a sudden he was ranting on about Tom Moody. Last words I heard was how he was going to make him pay for the death of his friend."

"Just what do you think he meant by that, Cook?" Colonel Spence asks.

Cook raises his eyebrows and draws his finger across his throat.

The colonel shakes his head. "That boy is hurting, so he's bound to be irrational, but he's no murderer. On the other hand, if he thinks he can go up against Moody and live to tell about it, he really has lost his mind. I'd better get word to Sheriff Redgrave to keep a watch for him."

"Well, Colonel, you know what they say about the apple not falling too far from the tree ..."

"I know what happened to the boy's father. But I know a mean-spirited man when I meet him, and that boy doesn't have it in him. Moody, on the other hand ..."

The station is quiet when Will hops off the afternoon train in Golden. Two tired bodies are curled up on the benches, dozing the time away. Maybe they are waiting for the westbound evening train, Will thinks. As he walks up Main Street, he cannot help but admire all the new buildings and businesses — like Smith's Dry Goods, the post office, and Dr. Mather's Medical Infirmary. Mother had written how Golden had become a real boom town.

But Will has another more important matter on his mind. He pulls his hat down low and keeps his eyes on the ground as he strides toward the Forrest House Saloon. With every step closer, the anger and hate inside him burn brighter.

Will is amazed how easy it was to find out where Moody had been holing up the past week. Then again, a man like Moody has a lot of enemies, and any one of them would be happy to offer a vengeful boy information and advice on how to handle the devil. But no matter how much those men hate Moody, none hates him as much as Will.

"You were right, Bennett," he whispers to himself as he bursts through the door of the Forrest House Saloon. "I should have stood up to the demon a long time ago."

No one knows who the angry young man is, nor pays him any attention. When Will's eyes adjust to the dimness, he glances around the smoky room. It does not take long for him to locate the hulk in the black corduroy jacket. He marches over to him while trying to plan his next move.

"You killed him, you merciless coward." The words fly out of Will's mouth before he has time to think.

Moody, who is in the middle of a card game and in deep concentration, does not raise his eyes. "I'll see your bet and raise you two bits, Collins."

Will repeats himself, even more agitated than before. "You're rotten to the core, Moody. And I know it was your fault that Bennett died. It was probably you who pulled the release on the box car that crushed him to death." Will notices there is a hush in the room now.

"Pay attention, Collins. What are you gonna do? Raise or fold? C'mon, I don't have all day."

Collins looks up at Will, whose fists are shaking and whose jaw is set harder than granite. Slowly, he puts down the playing cards and steps away from the table.

"What the … where are you going?" Moody finally glances up and sees the boy standing at his side. "What do you want? If you're here to play cards, then take a seat, otherwise get lost."

"I'm here to even the score for my friend, Bennett Robson," Will says fearlessly.

Moody takes another look at Will in the dim light and then his eyes widen. "Oh, it's you." He spits in disgust. "Take my advice, Irish. You best get yourself out of here while you can still walk. Otherwise I'll be wearing your rear end as a boot."

His laugh is more sinister than anything Will has ever heard. Without thinking, Will throws himself onto the hulk of a man, fists whirling like windmills. "You killed my best friend, you heartless fiend! How many others, Moody? How many others have you killed?"

With hardly any effort, Moody throws the boy to the floor. "Boy, those are awful strong words coming from the son of a murderer. People who live in glass houses ought not to throw stones is what I say. Your friend was an idiot who should've minded his own business."

At that moment the pale-faced barman steps forward. "Now look, Tom, I don't want any trouble in here. I want you and this here kid to get out and take your fight elsewhere. I don't want blood spilt on my floor, you hear? Now get out or I'm sending someone for the sheriff."

Moody narrows his eyes and rises from his seat. He towers over the bartender and looks big enough to pound him into the ground like a fence post. "All right, we'll finish this outside, Jimmy. But when I come back *my beer better still be here." Moody turns his black-bearded face to Will. "You heard him, boy."*

It has become painfully clear to Will that he has no next move. He drops his fists, and Moody grins, showing his black rotting teeth.

"Like the barman said, Maguire, we're going to take this fight outside, and I'm gonna finish it once and for all."

Moody turns and walks out of the saloon. Will follows, but grabs an empty glass beer bottle on his way.

Outside, Moody points to a pathway that runs alongside the Kicking Horse River. "That way, boy."

As the two get farther from the saloon, Will is aware that no one will see or hear anything — just what Moody wants. He realizes with a sickening numbness that these are probably his last steps, his last breaths, his last thoughts.

Moody laughs when he sees the bottle in Will's hand. "You think that's going to do it? I don't know how they ever convicted your old man for murder. He didn't have the guts for it and neither do you. That's because you're both spineless navvies." Moody whips out his new knife from his coat pocket and pulls off the sheath.

Just as before, the sunlight glints off the blade and nearly blinds Will. The boy's heart pumps so fast that it fills his mind and body with fear and courage. If this is his last day alive, then so be it, he thinks. But he will not die without a fight.

Rather than let Moody make the first move, Will raises the glass bottle and charges. At the same moment the heavy-set man lunges toward him, knife clenched in his fist. Will's one advantage is that his small size makes him quicker. As Moody's big arm comes down with full force, Will sidesteps him. Meeting no resistance, Moody's unchecked momentum hurls him toward the rock-lined embankment of the river. Like a boulder, he tumbles down the side and cracks his head again and again. Finally, he plunges into the powerful surging water.

Before Will can reach the river's edge, the huge, limp body is already rushing toward the mouth of the Columbia as easily as a stick riding on the surface. A few more seconds pass, and Thomas Moody is gone from sight altogether.

Stunned, Will climbs back up the riverbank to the pathway. He looks to the left and then to the right. In one direction is Golden, in the other a slim chance for freedom. With a large sigh, Will makes his decision and sorrowfully turns toward town to find the sheriff.

The Golden Era
Golden, British Columbia,
Saturday, July 21, 1892, Ten Cents

LOCAL MAN ARRESTED IN DEATH OF MINER

William Maguire was arrested for the murder of Thomas Moody. He will be tried in Kamloops at the assize court commencing on August 1, Justice Walkem presiding. Maguire is charged with willfully plotting the

---

death of the victim, whose body was dragged out of the river some eight miles from the scene of the crime. He possessed a cracked skull and was likely dead before entering the water. A number of witnesses have been summoned and will need to make the journey to Kamloops in due time. While inconvenient for citizens, a change of venue was a just action. If tried in Donald, it would be difficult to obtain an unprejudiced jury. At Kamloops that difficulty is not likely to occur, and the man should have a fair trial.

PROMINENT CITIZEN ANNOUNCES DAUGHTER'S ENGAGEMENT

Mr. Robert Heywood of Heywood's Hardware announced this past week the engagement of his eighteen-year-old daughter, Miss Rosie Heywood, to Mr. N. Murray. The father of the bride-to-be said his daughter will cease her popular millinery work once she is married and take up the role of wife and mother. Miss Heywood was not available for comment, but the groom, who is a widower and father of three, seemed very pleased with the arrangement. Reverend Cameron, uncle to Miss Heywood, will conduct the service.

EDITORIAL OPINION

"Oh, hell, you can't grow anything in this country!" is a remark often heard in Golden. It is uttered by men who know more about guzzling beer than they do about the capabilities of the soil they tread on. This opinion was formulated last Wednesday when this editor learned that another 16,000 empty beer bottles were shipped to Winnipeg. Rather than waste more time on the virtues of sobriety, a request is made to all good ladies to make the case for temperance and see to it that the men of this town find worthier pastimes, such as Bible reading.

The storm continued all Monday and into the next night. Environment Canada issued a warning to Golden residents to stay home if possible. When Mom heard about it on the news, she called to make sure I was safe. We talked for an hour, and I told her everything about the burial — the hangman's fracture, what I'd learned at the museum, and about Tristan, too. When Aunt Margaret got on the phone, all she wanted to know was if I'd been doing my school work.

"C'mon, Aunt Margaret, you know me. Nose in the books, shoulder to the grindstone. Work, work, work ..."

"Very funny, young lady. But you're right about one thing. I do know you, so I want you to hang up the phone and go do your homework."

"Yes, sir." I snapped a salute and stood at attention. Just then I heard Aunt Norma snickering in the kitchen.

On Tuesday morning the rain clouds thinned out and the wind finally turned into a breeze. Eddy called to say she had hired a couple of men who could help remove whatever mess had fallen onto the site.

"Roy and Arno will meet us there," Eddy said a half-hour later when she came to pick me up. "I don't mind telling you, Peggy, I'm pretty anxious about what we're going to find."

When we arrived at the old Pioneer Cemetery, there was no sign of the two workmen, but Eddy couldn't wait for them and shot up the hill toward the burial. I scrambled up behind her, tripping over branches, mud, and loose scree that had come down the hill.

"What the heck!" Eddy yelled.

I rushed to her side and stopped dead in my tracks. I could hardly believe what was there, or rather what wasn't there.

"Oh, my goodness, Peggy! It's gone, all of it, every last fragment."

Yup, she was right about that. There was nothing. What should have been a mound of tarps and hay and coffin and bones was nothing but a big hole half full of mud and rocks. "Eddy, did a mud slide somehow carry the coffin away?"

"No, Peggy. This isn't the work of the storm. Someone has deliberately removed the burial."

"But who could have done that? Who would even want to?"

Eddy sat on the ground and looked as if she'd just lost her dog. "There were only a few people who knew we were here excavating this burial," she mournfully insisted. "And of them only one who tried to steal it once before. I guess you were right all along. I've behaved like a fool and endangered the project. I'm going to have to go to the police now and tell them what Tristan has done."

CHAPTER TEN

What a mess things had turned into. We'd spent so much time and effort clearing the site, digging up buckets of earth, screening it, and then making an important discovery that nobody was going to learn about if we didn't find those remains.

I didn't think Eddy believed me when I said I didn't take any satisfaction in being right about Tristan. In fact, recent events and new information had left me rooting for the guy. More than anything I had hoped I would find new evidence that would clear his name.

When Eddy dropped me off at home, she told me to stay put until she talked to the police. She said they were going to want to speak to me after she made her report. Despite the seriousness of the matter, I took some delight in the image of the cop's face when Eddy told him that an entire burial had been stolen. How was he going to report it? Nameless human skeleton of undetermined age, race, and gender stolen from open hole in forgotten nineteenth-century cemetery.

Aunt Norma was out, so it was just Licorice and me ... again. As I sat on the sofa eating cheese and crackers, he actually seemed interested in me.

I soon realized it wasn't me, merely the cheese in my hand. In a gesture of friendship, I generously offered him a nibble.

"Ouch, Licorice that was my finger!" I yelped when he sank his teeth into me. As I yanked my hand back, he jumped off the sofa and hissed at me. Yes, the bloodthirsty feline actually hissed ... after biting me!

"Hey, Licorice, how'd you like to become guitar string?"

He did an about-face, and his tail sprang up like a pole. Then he sauntered off slowly, giving me a long look at his stiff-tailed behind. I'd bet anything that meant something rude in cat sign language.

After I finished my snack, I sat back to think through the whole situation. For the most part the vandalisms at the historic sites had all turned out to be pretty harmless stuff with a pretty big payoff. As for the burial in the Pioneer Cemetery, another long-forgotten piece of Golden history, what could that connection be? Could Tristan have simply been trying to wreck the burial? Nah. That was way too much work for an average teenager. And to dig up the entire thing during a storm ... well, that had to be completely beyond any vandal's work ethic.

Aunt Norma's folder with all her news stories was sitting on top of the coffee table. I leafed through it until I found the story on Tristan's arrest.

GOLDEN'S THIRD HISTORIC BURIAL DISTURBED — CULPRIT NABBED

RCMP received a tip at 11:00 p.m. on Saturday night that flashlights were seen and unusual activity heard coming from the hillside across the railway from the 7/11 store. Upon investigation, it was discovered that an unnamed minor was digging in what has since been identified as the abandoned Pioneer Cemetery.

"The boy was completely unremorseful when we caught him in the act," said Officer Skip Hopkins. "He denied being responsible for unlawfully disinterring the grave of this unfortunate Golden citizen. With a shovel in hand he told me, 'This is not what it appears to be.' Of course, I didn't believe him. After all, he was caught in the act."

The teen is known to police, who believe him to be the same person responsible for the chain of vandalism occurring to historic burials and sites around town. The provincial Archaeology Branch has been contacted and will send a specialist to assess the situation and likely excavate the burial that dates to the late 1800s.

Because the accused is a minor, charges are pending. A decision from the court will be made after consultation with the Archaeology Branch representative.

It sounded pretty cut and dried. One no-good teenager responsible for wrecking a bunch of neglected historic sites that now happened to be in better shape than ever before, plus one heroic nutball police officer who led the restoration and became a hero to history buffs worldwide.

My mind kept returning to the expression on Officer Hopkins's face when he told me about Tristan's mom abandoning him. He didn't appear to be the slightest bit sympathetic. In fact, he seemed harsh. And when Tristan got caught that night, what had he meant by *this is not what it looks like*? If it wasn't supposed to look like a teenage vandal wrecking an old forgotten burial, then what was it?

I was beginning to see too many loose ends in this whole scenario. And even though Eddy had asked me to stay home, I had a strong urge to talk to Uncle Henry. I was pretty sure he could help make sense of things. And if Tristan did steal the remains, he might know of a reason why he'd do it and where he'd stash them.

When I arrived at the museum, it was locked again. This time I ran around to the back. After seeing Uncle Henry's car, I banged on the door. When I didn't get an answer, I shimmied up the drainpipe and peered through a tiny window. The lights were on, but I couldn't see anyone. Just as I was about to jump down, Uncle Henry came into the room wearing his white gloves.

"Uncle Henry, Uncle Henry!" I cried, banging loudly on the window. "Please let me in. I need to talk to you." After the shock of seeing me in the window wore off, I got the feeling from his furrowed brows that he wasn't happy to see me. When he finally came to the door, he only opened it a crack.

"I'm sorry, Peggy, but the museum is closed today. I have important work to get caught up on. Please come back tomorrow and visit." He tried closing the door, but I stuck my boot inside the crack.

"Uncle Henry," I said, "I need to ask you some questions. Do you think Tristan's the type who would deliberately ruin historic sites?"

He dropped his hand and sighed deeply. "Not at all, Peggy. Samuel is a good boy."

"But he was caught in the act, Uncle Henry. And from the police's point of view it makes sense to link him to the other vandalism, too."

Uncle Henry shook his head sadly.

"What's even worse now is that the burial, the one Tristan was caught digging up, has been stolen. And just when it was revealing some important information."

Uncle Henry's eyes opened wide. "Important information, you say. Like what?"

"The guy was executed, Uncle Henry. Eddy says she's never seen a case of hangman's fracture like this in her life. And as I'm sure you know, back then only people convicted of first-degree murder were hanged. He must have been a real rotten tomato, and when I was here yesterday, I was trying to discover his identity."

Uncle Henry pulled me into the room and shut the door quickly. "Unfortunately, I didn't get to finish the story of my family yesterday. But if you were looking for information about the hanged man, why didn't you just ask me?"

That caught me off guard. "Well, okay, then, I'm asking you now. Can you show me anything you've got on the guy who was hanged and buried in the Pioneer Cemetery? And by the way, what's your family story got to do with it?"

"The boy who was buried in the cemetery was William Maguire."

"William Maguire? But that was your uncle. The one you said saved the family from ruin after your grandfather was sent to jail." I searched for a chair to sit down on. I had a feeling this was going to be a long story.

He sighed again. "Yes, that's him."

"So Uncle William's a killer?"

Uncle Henry's eyes turned grave, and his mouth narrowed into a tiny frown. "He was no killer, Peggy."

I guffawed and slapped my leg. "Well, they didn't just hang him for being a jaywalker, you know. The guy was arrested, tried by a jury, and then convicted for premeditated murder. That's not the kind of thing that happens to good people."

"I can't speak for other people, but in Uncle William's case I can assure you he didn't deserve to be executed. He may or may not have been the cause of another man's death, but I'll tell you one thing, my father never believed William meant to kill anyone and said the proof was buried with his brother."

"Proof? What kind of proof?"

"Uncle William wrote a letter to his mother the night before his death and told her everything. For some reason she buried the letter with him. My father believed it would clear any question of William's guilt. With all the new interest in our town's past, it seemed like a good time to bring attention to the long-forgotten Pioneer Cemetery, to find that letter, to prove once and for all that Uncle William wasn't a killer, and to clear the Maguire name."

When the penny finally dropped, I felt my brain burp. "Are you saying it was you who put Tristan up to some plan to dig up your uncle's burial in the Pioneer Cemetery?"

"No," said an angry voice behind me. Tristan came out of the small room. He was wearing the same white gloves as Uncle Henry. "He didn't put me up to anything. As someone who knows what it's like to be blamed for every broken window and stolen car, I had my own reasons for wanting to prove William's innocence."

Tristan looked different. The black eyeliner was gone, there was no nose ring, and he wasn't speaking in Shakespeare quotes or a phony British accent.

"Samuel, the time for truth is upon us. Peggy, I was going to do it alone. Samuel tried to convince me to stop, but when I wouldn't he insisted on helping me."

"And the other sites — was that you, too?" I asked.

Uncle Henry's cheeks turned pink, and his hands began to shake. "Yes, me, too, I'm afraid. It was the only way to bring attention to those neglected historic sites. Citizens of Golden had forgotten the people who made this a great town. I'd tried for years to get our elected officials to put money into keeping the sites up and to educate the public. But no one cared, not until they'd been vandalized, that is. And thanks to your aunt, they became news items."

"That's right," Tristan said. "After that, people began to take an interest. Even that puffed-up airhead Constable Hop-a-Long got involved and spearheaded a volunteer committee."

Uncle Henry nodded. "Yes, and citizens became curious about these people's places in our history. They even began visiting the museum again."

"But, Uncle Henry, you broke the law," I said. "I'm not talking about some broken grammar rule. You actually committed a crime."

"The law can be wrong sometimes," Tristan said. "Look what it did to William."

"No, Samuel, Peggy is correct. I did break the law, and I'm prepared to suffer the consequences, as soon as I've had the chance to examine the letter that will prove William's innocence."

I got an instantaneous picture in my mind that sent a tingle up the back of my neck. "Uncle Henry, you have the burial here, don't you?" I whispered as though saying it out loud might get me in trouble.

He turned and beckoned me to follow him to the back of the museum where there was a small room with two large rectangular tables. On one was the dry, crumbling skeleton, and on the other the coffin that had once held the remains.

As I gazed at those bones, I had a growing feeling of melancholy. Maybe that was because I'd seen his young, proud face and had heard the sad story of his life and knew his name now — William Maguire. He was barely more than a kid when he went to work in the mines to help his mother and little brother and sister. He was only eighteen years old when he died at the end of a rope alone, without family or a single friend at his side.

Uncle Henry broke into my silence. "We were just about to examine the contents of this leather pouch, Peggy. My father told me that Uncle William's letter would hold the key to proving his innocence. This is the day we find out."

I wasn't sure what I should do. I didn't want to become an accomplice to their crime. Fortunately, I didn't have to make a choice, because we all heard the sound of sirens coming from outside the museum. A few seconds later Officer Hopkins, Eddy, and Aunt Norma burst through the doorway.

"Peggy, what are you doing here?" Aunt Norma asked, her mouth gaping.

Before I could ask her the same question, Officer Skippy pushed past me. "There you are! I'm taking you into custody, boy! What did you do with that burial?"

Tristan didn't even try to run. In fact, he was completely calm. "Right in here, Officer." He led them into the next room to see the remains on the table. That was when Officer Skippy reached out and slapped handcuffs on Tristan's wrists.

"Wait a minute, Skip," Aunt Norma snapped. "Don't you think you're missing something here?"

Skippy stopped and looked around.

"The burial remains are sitting here in Henry's lab," Aunt Norma pointed out.

"That's right, Officer," Uncle Henry said. "If you're going to arrest Samuel, then you might as well arrest me, too."

"Wait a minute," Aunt Norma insisted. "Before you haul anyone off to jail, it might be a good idea to ask some questions. Don't you think?"

I wasn't sure if it was because Aunt Norma was ticked off at him, or whether it was because she'd just stated the obvious, but Officer Skippy's face suddenly turned a splendid shade of "I'm-so-embarrassed" red. I wanted to giggle, but instead I bit my lip and remained quiet.

"Well, you might have a point there, Miss Johnson." Officer Hopkins turned and faced Uncle Henry. "I'm very disappointed that you're mixed up with all this, Mr. Murphy. So you'd better explain why this burial is in the museum lab and how it got here."

It took a while for Uncle Henry to explain how with Tristan's help he had managed to dig up the entire burial and coffin in a major storm and bring it to the museum. Eddy was almost giddy when he told everyone the remains were of his Uncle William. When he finished the story, he lifted the leather pouch for all to see.

Eddy's eyes lit up. "Where did you get that?"

"It was located beneath the lace pillow under the skull," Uncle Henry said. "I knew it would be there. My father told me about it long ago."

"Have you examined the contents?" Eddy asked.

Uncle Henry's voice trembled. "I was just going to before you all arrived. I've waited my whole life to look inside this pouch. So if you'll tolerate my behaviour a little longer and allow me to read the contents of the letter, I'll be eternally grateful, Dr. McKay and Officer Hopkins."

Officer Skippy's chest puffed up like a rooster's, and he had that all-too-familiar smug look on his face. "I'm sorry, Mr. Murphy. You've broken the law." He took Uncle Henry's arm and began ushering him to the door along with Tristan.

"Oh, stop it, Skip!" Aunt Norma's lip curled into a sneer. "Give us a break, will you?"

Wow! I'd just witnessed any chance Officer Hopkins had to date my aunt go up in smoke. By the look on his face, I think he knew it, too.

"Officer, as I see it, Tristan and Mr. Murphy have done me and the Provincial Archaeology Branch a service, albeit an unusual one, and one not to be repeated, I'm sure," Eddy said. "You see, when the weather warning came, I tried everything in my power to find someone to come and safely remove the burial before it was damaged by the storm. As I see it, that's been accomplished, and at a great savings to the department." She smiled gently at Uncle Henry. "Remind me later to get more details on how you managed to do it."

"Now wait a minute," Officer Skippy protested. "If I get you right, you're suggesting we let these two get away with breaking the law?"

"No, no, no, not at all, Officer. What I'm saying is they've done exactly what I wanted and have safely removed the burial to this laboratory before the storm damaged it. Had I known they were trying to be of service I would never have bothered you." It looked as if Officer Skippy was tongue-tied. "And by the way, Mr. Murphy, it looks like you've done a top-notch job. I'll now be able to continue my examination from the safety of this laboratory."

"But —" Skippy tried to interject.

"Officer Hopkins, no charges will be laid," Eddy said. "Not by me or the Archaeology Branch. Please remove the handcuffs from the boy."

Tristan wore a smirk that I was sure was going to get him into hot water down the road.

"Now," Eddy continued, "since that's all settled, Mr. Murphy, as the archaeologist in charge of this excavation, I suggest we take a look at the contents of that leather pouch."

"Right on!" I blurted. Everyone turned and looked at me. "Oops, there I go again. Gotta remember to get myself a muzzle one of these days." I glanced at Tristan, whose eyebrows spoke volumes. "Don't say a word!"

Uncle Henry placed the weathered old pouch onto a stainless-steel tray. Then Eddy put on some white gloves and gently unfolded the stiff leather flap. While she held it in place, Uncle Henry used some oversized tweezers to pull out the ancient yellowed paper slowly. As we all watched wide-eyed, including Officer Skippy, he carefully unfolded the letter. Up until that moment I hadn't realized I'd been holding my breath, and suddenly it came out in one huge swoosh.

"For crying out loud, Peggy," bellowed Aunt Norma. "You nearly made me faint."

Uncle Henry used the magnifying glass to examine the page more carefully. He seemed to take forever, and just when I thought I couldn't stand it any longer, he finally glanced up.

"Well, what does it say?" Tristan asked before I could pose the same question.

Uncle Henry exhaled deeply. "Nothing."

"Nothing!" I cried. "What do you mean nothing? Does it say William was innocent or not?"

"It doesn't say either because the paper is much too deteriorated and the ink has faded beyond the point of reading the words." Uncle Henry was pale, and Tristan helped him to a chair. "After all these years of hoping, the letter hasn't solved anything. I'm back to where I started — with no proof of Uncle

William's innocence." Uncle Henry sighed heavily, then blew his nose on his handkerchief. "After all I've put you through, Samuel, I'm sorry." Tristan put his hand on his friend's shoulder.

"Mr. Murphy, I see you're very disappointed," Eddy said. "But maybe this will make you feel better." She handed him a small gold object. It wasn't until Uncle Henry opened it that I saw it was an old-fashioned pocket watch.

"Where ... where did you get this?" he asked with new energy.

"It was at the bottom of the pouch. I found it while you were examining the letter. Take a look at what it says on the lid and tell me if it means anything to you."

He picked up the magnifying glass and began to read aloud slowly. "'For William, a devoted and self-less son. Love, Father and Mother.'"

I didn't know if anyone felt like me, but those words made my heart go numb and my eyes sting.

A moment later Uncle Henry sat up straight. He had a new glow on his face. "It's dated June 19, 1892 — that was William's eighteenth birthday."

"Maybe you didn't get the answers you'd been hoping for, Uncle Henry," I said. "But I think this confirms something you already knew. William Maguire was a loyal and brave boy who sacrificed everything for his family. He took on one of the hardest jobs any human being ever had to endure to support his mother and little brother and sister. And when Thomas Moody died, maybe because of him, William didn't run away. No, he turned himself in and let the court decide his fate." I realized at that moment how much Tristan's life had been like William's. "If you ask me, he was a good person who didn't deserve to be hanged."

Uncle Henry smiled. "Well, Samuel, what do you think? Do you agree with Peggy?"

Tristan's cheeks had become rosy, and his eyes were moist. "Uncle Henry, there's nothing either good nor bad, but thinking makes it so."

I immediately recognized the quote I'd first seen on Aunt Norma's wall the night I had arrived in Golden. For once I really wanted to know what Shakespeare meant, but before I had a chance to ask, Tristan explained.

"Just as beauty is in the eye of the beholder, I'd say goodness was, too. Each one of us will have to decide in our own minds whether William was a hero or a cad. Personally, I agree with Peggy and believe he must have been a great guy."

I smiled back. "Mr. Shakespeare, I'm glad we finally agree on something."

Thursday, September 15, 1892

Dear Mama,

My jailer granted my request for pen and paper and promised this letter will be delivered. By now you are in full knowledge of the events that led to my present predicament. I am sorrier than you can ever imagine. I only hope Father has been spared this knowledge, for I fear it will lead him to act rashly.

I need not tell you the contents of my heart the day I went to Moody. Only that the hatred I felt was fuelled by the loss of my only true friend. In the end, even that could never make me take another man's life. But you know me better than anyone, and how I have always lived by the rule, "To thine own self be true." Unfortunately, this virtue has not saved my life. Perhaps there is hope for my soul.

My only fear on this eve before my death is for you, Henry and Emily. Colonel Spence will send the last of my pay along to you soon. With that and the money my gold pocket watch will fetch, you should be able to manage for a while.

Mama, it is time you sold the land and started a new life. There is nothing left for you in Golden except sorrowful memories and broken dreams.

When you think of me, please remember only the better days.

Your eternally loving son,
Will

CHAPTER ELEVEN

It was our last day in Golden, and before Eddy and I left for home, I needed to visit the museum one last time. As I strolled in, Uncle Henry was talking to some visitors.

"Golden was a raucous and dangerous town back in those days, but if a person liked excitement and adventure, then it was the place to be," he said proudly. "Now, may I suggest you begin your tour in the town's original train station located behind the museum? It was constructed during the early 1880s when the CPR was building the railway across Canada. Originally, it was located next to our Pioneer Cemetery, but was brought to this location about fifty years ago to preserve for future generations."

Uncle Henry was in his element. It made me happy to know that Eddy had recommended that the town council should appoint him Golden's honorary historic site keeper. I was glad that Tristan was his second-in-command, too — and new roommate.

"Peggy, it was good of you to come by," Uncle Henry said when the couple had gone to see the train station. "You know I'm going to miss our visits."

"Me, too, Uncle Henry. I hope it's okay if I finish my research for my school report today."

"Yes, yes, come this way. I have just what you need." I followed him into the office where he handed me a pair of white gloves. After I put them on, he gave me *The Golden Era*. "This is the last of William's story. I think you'll find it interesting."

I sat at the table and brushed my hand over the weathered newspaper to flatten it out gently. As I turned the pages that were like dry petals, my white-gloved fingertips became soiled by the nearly one hundred and thirty years of dust that had collected on the surface. I began to read the news entry slowly, savouring every last detail of William's life.

The Golden Era
Golden, British Columbia,
Saturday, September 24, 1892, Ten Cents

FATHER AND SON BURIED
SIDE BY SIDE

A handful of Golden citizens braved the nasty rainstorm to attend the funeral of the convicted murderer, William Maguire, and his father. Aside from the immediate family, which included Mrs. Maguire and her two youngest children, there was Sheriff Redgrave and Mrs. Potts in attendance. Reverend Cameron presided over the solemnities.

Like his father, the younger Maguire was convicted of murder. Maguire senior was responsible for the death of esteemed Golden citizen, David Craig, in July 1888. Unlike the son, Kenneth Maguire committed a crime that was an irrational act of anger. But William was judged to have premeditated the killing of a miner by the name of Thomas Moody and was hanged on September 17 at the Kamloops gaol.

A sick twist in the plot of this tragic story was when Maguire senior was shot dead while trying to escape from the provincial penitentiary in New Westminster. It is speculated he was trying to get to his son before the execution. Maguire junior knew nothing of his father's death prior to his own hanging, which may be the only small blessing in the whole rotten tale.

Now that the Maguire farm is up for sale and the remaining family members are departing, let us hope that this brings an end to this tragic tale — for their sake and for the sake of the town of Golden. As for father and son, their remains will lay forever side by side, and may their souls bring each other comfort.

GOLDEN IN NEED OF NEW CEMETERY

Sheriff Redgrave announced that Golden is in need of a new cemetery. He said the existing one has reached its capacity and will not serve the community for much longer. The search is on to find a suitable location for the new town cemetery. The sheriff said with any luck the Maguire men will be the last to be buried in this location. This writer assumes the luck the sheriff was speaking of was not in the finding of new property but in the hopes that Golden will not be burying any more of its citizens anytime soon.

That line about father and son being side by side forever was a real heart squeezer. From what Eddy had said about the subsurface radar, I knew there were human remains buried next to William's. But I would never have guessed it was his father's burial. I closed the old newspaper and gently refolded it.

Sitting quietly, I thought how things could have been different for William and his family if people had helped instead of judging and turning their backs on them. I guess I couldn't say for sure if I'd have been any better. Look how I had treated Tristan! But at least I now got what Eddy had said about how sometimes good people do bad things and that I should condemn the action and not the person.

"There's one thing I wanted to ask," I said when Uncle Henry returned to the room. "Why is your last name Murphy instead of Maguire?"

He shrugged. "I suppose that after Uncle William's death Grandmother wanted to start a new life. She sold the farm, began using her maiden name, which was Murphy, and then moved away. But probably the most important reason she changed it was to protect her children from the judgment and suspicion the Maguire name was sure to have."

"So how did you end up living here in Golden, Uncle Henry?"

"My father swore he would return one day. He said Golden was his home and he wanted to be near his father and brother. So when he grew up, he came back here, lived a good and peaceful life, raised a family, and was a model citizen."

"How did you find out about your uncle and grandfather? Did it shock you?"

Uncle Henry chuckled. "Oh, no, I grew up hearing the stories of my Uncle William and my grandfather. Despite the fact they'd done some very bad things, my father knew that at heart they were good men. You have to remember that the times were rough and people survived by being tough, too. And even long after the Pioneer Cemetery had been forgotten, my father and I visited the graves of our relatives, brought flowers, said prayers." At that moment the visitors returned and looked eager to ask questions. "Excuse me, Peggy, duty calls."

I was glad to have some time to think. I let all the details of the past ten days sift through my mind like a screen separating the earth from tiny, missed artifacts. I thought about all of William's broken bones. They were like small symbols that told the story of broken hearts and dreams, and of what might have been, but never was.

"Mrs. Maguire, you have my deepest sympathy for your loss." Sheriff Redgrave tips his hat respectfully. "Reverend Cameron reports that the graves are prepared. We can begin anytime you're ready, ma'am."

Suzanna Maguire nods. "Come, dears, it's time."

Emily's tear-stained face is buried in her mother's arms. When she snivels, her brother reaches out with his handkerchief to wipe her nose. Suzanna smiles at this gesture.

"May I escort you up the hill?" the sheriff asks Suzanna.

"You're very kind, Sheriff Redgrave. I would be grateful for a steady arm to lean on."

Suzanna rests her gloved hand on the sheriff's outstretched arm. The chilly wind and heavy rain punish the few mourners who have gathered this morning to pay their last respects to William and Kenneth Maguire. While Emily and her mother begin the climb toward the graves, Henry lingers behind. He turns to the train tracks so no one will see him brush the tears away, especially his mother. She says he is the man of the family now, and men are not supposed to cry, even if they are only fourteen. Henry recalls William was his same age when he became the man of the family, too, and left home to work in the mines.

"Come along, Henry, it's time to say our last good-byes," Suzanna calls after him.

Although the cemetery is small, it holds many of Golden's citizens. As Suzanna passes the many white crosses, she pauses by the white fence surrounding David Craig's grave and feels an extra wave of heaviness. All their troubles seemed to start with him. She notices there are fresh flowers, a reminder of his widow's recent visit. But she does not allow her thoughts to linger long on such matters, for she must lay her own loved ones to rest.

As the mourners gather around the freshly dug pits, the orientation of the plain wooden boxes holding the remains of father and son does not go unnoticed. It was Reverend Cameron who instructed the pallbearers to place them as such, so that they will never see the rising sun on Judgment Day. Suzanna thinks it is a cruel final gesture to deprive these two souls of their everlasting peace. As her chest heaves and her lips tremble, she fights with all her might not to allow the floodgates of her emotions to open wide. She must not allow it for Henry's and Emily's sakes. Steady, Suzanna, she tells herself. Steady.

The words offered by the preacher are brief and lack any Christian comfort. Even Sheriff Redgrave shifts uncomfortably under the weight of such an unsympathetic eulogy. At the finish Suzanna leans into the coffin of her eldest son and traces the soft auburn curls on his forehead with her finger. At last she tucks a small package under the lacy pillow that holds his dear young head.

"William, you've been a good and generous son. And Mama wants you to have these things — they belong to you." She touches her fingertips to her lips and sends her son a final kiss.

Soon the mourners silently make their way back down the pathway, leaving behind William and Kenneth to their black holes of gloom.

Sheriff Redgrave takes Suzanna Maguire by the arm and walks her along the road toward town and the train station where the family's trunks await. "I am truly sorry to see it come to this, Mrs. Maguire. Despite all that has transpired, I feel certain Kenneth and William were good men caught up in an inescapable trap."

"Thank you, Sheriff. When Kenneth and I brought our family to Golden, we thought we had found the land of our dreams, but it was not to be and we became nothing but slaves to it. In return for our toil, sweat, and tears, all we got was a damp and cold log shack, nights of going to bed in hunger, and despair that ate our souls year after year. Today there is scarcely anyone who can look on us or speak the Maguire name without thinking horribly of us all. Our life here in Golden is finished, and it is time to begin again."

Suzanna wipes the corner of her eyes with her tiny handkerchief. Off in the distance they hear the

rhythmic chugs and hiss of the train as it draws closer.
Then the whistle blows, announcing the mighty CPR
engine is yet again on time.

I smoothed the old newspaper and gently inserted
it back in the stack. In some ways I felt melancholy
that our work was over and we were leaving. But I
was also looking forward to getting home to Mom,
Uncle Stuart, and yes, even Aunt Margaret. When I
talked to them on the phone the night before, Aunt
Margaret reminded me about my homework assign-
ments. I told her I was writing a paper on Golden's
history and the archaeological excavation we did —
a two-for-one deal, you could say.

"I'm calling it 'All That Glistens Is Not Golden,'"
I said. "In case you didn't get it, Aunt Margaret,
that's a pun on something Shakespeare wrote in his
play *The Merchant of Venice*. My friend Sam helped
me to come up with that."

Yeah, I was starting to get goofy about Shakespeare, too — definitely a sign it was time to return to
the present and home.

I picked up my backpack and headed out the
door of the little museum. Quickly, I glanced at the
old train station sitting at the back of the property.
For a moment I pictured the last of the Maguires,
ready to leave behind their broken hearts and broken dreams and board the train that would take
them to a new life.

When one of the little gophers scampered across the lawn, I remembered that Tristan, I mean, Sam, was meeting me at Aunt Norma's. Before Eddy and I got on the road, we were all going to visit the wolves at Northern Lights Wolf Sanctuary. It was Aunt Norma's idea. She insisted we do something "normal" for once. I took off down Front Street, heading for home.

AUTHOR'S NOTE

While *Broken Bones* involves mainly fictitious characters and events, it takes place in Golden, one of British Columbia's oldest communities. The area was first visited in 1807 by explorer David Thompson, though it was long known to the Shuswap First Nations people.

Golden, like so many tent cities that grew up as the Canadian Pacific Railway was being built, was truly the Wild West. As the province matured, there was a need to bring law and order to small towns like Golden. Judge Matthew Begbie, Sam Steele, and Sheriff Stephen Redgrave were historic figures who were part of an early law-enforcement effort and have since become Canadian icons.

There are a number of actual historic events alluded to in *Broken Bones*. Some were taken right from the pages of old-town newspapers like Donald's *The Truth* and Golden's *The Golden Era*. For instance, I was intrigued by the murder of William Archer by Michael Kennedy in 1888. I used that case and all the details connected to it to create elements of my own story.

The style of writing for small-town newspapers was distinct and written mostly by men who were highly opinionated, often racist, and chauvinistic. While today's journalists try to be objective in their reporting, these small-town newspaper editors often had free rein to write whatever they wanted. I tried to copy this style of writing and occasionally included actual news articles such as the building of the first Sikh temple in North America in Golden.

An archaeological investigation was conducted at the Golden Pioneer Cemetery in 1988 and 1989 by scientists from Simon Fraser University. Ms. Lindsey Oliver wrote her master's thesis on this excavation project. Her report was rich with details and very helpful in the writing of this story. The detailed descriptions of the human remains were proof that those were violent and dangerous times. Many of these details were incorporated into this novel such as the knife wound on one individual's femur and the crushed vertebrae of the lower back on another.

Finally, the little museum in Golden was another invaluable source of information. For historical archaeologists, written documentation, integrated with artifacts and other physical evidence, helps to create a more complete picture of past human behaviour. And that is ultimately the goal of archaeology — to know as much as we can about the people who lived long ago.

Also by
Gina McMurchy-Barber

Reading the Bones
A Peggy Henderson Adventure
978-1550027327
$11.99

Due to circumstances beyond her control, twelve-year-old Peggy Henderson has to move to the quiet town of Crescent Beach, British Columbia, to live with her aunt and uncle. Without a father and separated from her mother, who's looking for work, Peggy feels her unhappiness increasing until the day she and her uncle start digging a pond in the backyard and she realizes the rock she's been trying to pry from the ground is really a human skull.

Peggy eventually learns that her home and the entire seaside town were built on top of a five-thousand-year-old Coast Salish fishing village. With the help of an elderly archaeologist, a woman named Eddy, Peggy comes to know the ancient storyteller buried in her yard in a way that few others can — by reading the bones.

As life with her aunt becomes more and more unbearable, Peggy looks to the old Salish man from the past for help and answers.

Free as a Bird
Governor General's Literary Award Finalist in 2010!
978-1554884476
$12.99

Born with Down syndrome, Ruby Jean Sharp comes from a time when being a developmentally disabled person could mean growing up behind locked doors and barred windows and being called names like "retard" and "moron." When Ruby Jean's caregiver and loving grandmother dies, her mother takes her to Woodlands School in New Westminster, British Columbia, and rarely visits.

As Ruby Jean herself says: "Can't say why they called it a school — a school's a place you go for learnin an then after you get to go home. I never learnt much bout ledders and numbers, an I sure never got to go home."

It's here in an institution that opened in 1878 and was originally called the Provincial Lunatic Asylum that Ruby Jean learns to survive isolation, boredom, and every kind of abuse. Just when she can hardly remember if she's ever been happy, she learns a lesson about patience and perseverance from an old crow.

Available at your favourite bookseller.

MIX
Paper from
responsible sources
FSC® C004071